12/15/09

TRAIN TO CHEYENNE

In Memory of:
Betsy Snyder
by
Rebecca Baker

TRAIN TO CHEYENNE

•

David Unruh

AVALON BOOKS
NEW YORK

Published by Thomas Bouregy & Co., Inc.
160 Madison Avenue, New York, NY 10016

Library of Congress Cataloging-in-Publication Data

Unruh David.
   Train to Cheyenne / David Unruh.
        p. cm.
   ISBN 978-0-8034-9991-1 (acid-free paper)
   1. Train robberies—Fiction.   I. Title.
   PS3621.N67T73 2009
   813'.6—dc22

                                        2009024473

PRINTED IN THE UNITED STATES OF AMERICA
ON ACID-FREE PAPER
BY HADDON CRAFTSMEN, BLOOMSBURG, PENNSYLVANIA

Thanks to my wife, Carol, and my daughter, Kristine, for reading my novels and giving gentle, encouraging criticism.

Chapter One

Nate Jackson stepped out onto the porch of his small house in Omaha and took a deep breath. There was still time to back out, to return to his house, sit with his wife in their front room, and listen to her chatter about what she had done during the day. She needed a new dress, his daughter had learned something new in school, the kitchen door needed fixing, or other news in which he had diminishing interest. He cleared his mind and walked to the street.

Working for Humphrey Hopkins, the Omaha banker, had never been easy for Nate. He had come to Omaha at the end of the Civil War and thought that banking in the railroad boom-town would be a way to secure a future of wealth and re-spectability. But Hopkins was intolerant, demanding, and stingy. And now, after four years of faithful service, Nate found himself having to share his office with Hopkins' nephew, who was dedicated and eager to prove to his uncle how superior he was to Nate.

His house was five blocks from the bank where he worked, but he was not in a particular hurry. It was seven in the evening on a fine spring Friday in 1870; he had left work an hour before, an hour after the nephew, Stephen Hopkins. He had no legitimate need nor any justification to return to his office, but he was dressed in his bank teller's clothes, as if he were heading to work on any weekday morning. After looking at his watch and fingering the keys in his pocket, he strode toward downtown Omaha.

Tied to a tree in a grove on an undeveloped lot nearby was a horse he had hired from the livery stable. It was his decoy, part of his plan. After removing what he knew to be over five thousand in gold from the bank, he would take the horse to the river under cover of darkness and kill it, letting it fall into the river and float away, hopefully to sink in the mud downstream. The authorities would discover that he had hired a horse and tack and assume he was headed cross-country. After disposing of the horse, he would have just enough time to board the stern-wheeler that was due to cast off at nine that evening, headed for St. Louis.

There was an alley that led to the back door of the bank, and he used this route to approach the building. It would not be in his interest to expose himself to being seen from the street. He didn't want to chat with anyone; he didn't want to nod politely to them on the street; he didn't want to be seen at all if he could help it.

There was no one in the alley, and he walked undetected

to the back door. He quickly inserted his key, opened the door, stepped in, and closed the door behind himself, wincing slightly as the heavy latch snapped noisily back into place.

The fading evening light was adequate for him to work the combination on the large safe, and in minutes he had it open. He pulled out the express box and set it on Hopkins' desk. It felt light, too light to have gold in it. There should be a key in the banker's desk.

Banker Hopkins, whose sole mission in life seemed to be to make Nate Jackson's life more miserable. Hopkins, the fat old man who, although wealthy by any standard, was too stingy to pay Nate Jackson a wage that would enable him and his needy wife to live in the style they both thought they deserved. (It was one of the few things Nate and his wife agreed upon, that they should have more income.) Hopkins, who made a great show of going to church every Sunday but was mean, greedy, demanding, and intolerant.

Humphey Hopkins—whose spoiled nephew unfortunately chose that moment to walk in the front door of the bank and catch Nate Jackson in the process of searching his uncle's desk for the key to the express box.

"Nathan," he said, "why are you here at this time of the evening?"

Nate jumped and looked at Stephen Hopkins in surprise.

"And what are you doing with the express box?"

There was no answer Nate could think of that would explain the circumstances. His surprise gave way to anger. Illogically he thought to himself, what right did this man have to interrupt what should have been an easy crime? True to Nate's opinion of him, Hopkins—and, by proxy, his nephew—was again spoiling something for him.

Stephen walked to Nate and stood directly in front of him, staring up at the taller man's face. "My God, man, what's going on here?"

Nate was raging inside. He backed up a step, and his hand found the empty coatrack. He grabbed it and swung it at Stephen. Stephen went down and tried to cover his head with his arms. Nate kicked him hard in the stomach, and then, when Stephen lowered his arms to protect his stomach, Nate hit him again in the head, now wielding the coatrack with both hands for more power. The nephew cried for mercy; Nate hit him again, and he was silent.

Nate resumed rifling Hopkins' desk but found no key. He lifted the box again. He shook it. He was more than ever sure that there was no gold in the box. Then he went to the safe and scooped each shelf clean, finding only bank records, deeds, and various papers of importance but of no value to him. A fury was building in him that took all his self-control to subdue. He kicked at some of the scattered papers he had thrown to the floor and cursed Hopkins. Stephen moaned but made no attempt to get to his feet.

Nate got his emotions under control and sat at Hopkins' desk. How could he salvage this situation? He could kill Stephen and then slip back to his house in the darkness. He could set fire to the bank. But where was the profit? Even if the arson concealed his crime, he would be back where he had been, except that he might no longer have a job. And he would still be in Omaha. And still have a wife and child.

Something was wrong. There was no gold; the week's deposits were missing; there was nothing. The express box should have held gold, and the safe should have contained the week's deposits—wealth sufficient to support him in whatever enterprise he might start back East where he had grown up. Now his dreams of a better life might slip away.

Nate opened each drawer of Hopkins' desk. He had to pry one open, splintering the wood. There was nothing of interest except a small revolver. Hopkins would never leave any amount of money in a wooden desk; he was too careful with money. Nate went to the still-motionless nephew and removed his wallet. At least it had sixty-five dollars in it. He stuffed the cash into his pocket and then pulled a ring from Stephen's finger and a gold watch from his pocket. Stephen offered no resistance.

In his haste to find the gold, Nate had scattered his teller's drawer on the floor. There were only small bills and pocket change, but he picked those up and pocketed them also—a very poor return for all of his scheming.

Nate had the presence of mind to think of one other thing: the currency shipments to the Army outposts on the railroad. He looked through Hopkins' correspondence until he found the shipping schedule and added that to the cash he had stolen. That was that. A few hundred dollars, some jewelry, a loaded revolver, and information that might or might not be valuable. The start of Nate Jackson's criminal career was inauspicious.

Nate left the bank undetected and found his horse in the grove of trees. He could use the horse to make a getaway to the West, but there was very little in the way of civilization in that direction, and few opportunities to improve his situation. Riding across the plains to California or Santa Fe held no appeal and, in fact, frightened him a little. Plus, he had no bedroll and no food.

He could follow his original plan—kill the horse and board the stern-wheeler—and that seemed the safest escape. But his few hundred dollars would not last long on the Missouri River or the Mississippi. By the time he reached New Orleans, he would be in need of more money.

If he wanted to try to intercept an express shipment, he needed to stay close to the rail line. He had one person in Omaha he could trust, his brother. Together they might still be able to realize profit from his bungled bank robbery.

Nate led the horse to a swampy area near the river. The brush was thick there and with luck would hide the carcass for a long time. It would be assumed he had headed west, and there would be reward posters dispatched in that direction. In the meantime he could find a place to hide for a few weeks and make a new plan.

Chapter Two

"Bull," the policeman said at the window, "here comes that kid again."

Bull didn't look up from his desk. "Is he wearing a gun?"

"Yeah," the policeman answered.

"All right. Is he coming here?"

"Looks like it."

The chief sighed. The young man approaching his office had been hanging around for several months. He couldn't help but like him, and he was flattered that the boy had taken such an interest in law enforcement, but he sensed a lack of maturity. He thought the boy was not yet able to see the real world the way an older man would. This was worrisome. There was a light tap on the office door.

"Come on in, Jimmy," the chief said loudly.

The door opened, and Jimmy Whipwell stepped into the

room. He removed his hat and then waited for a few seconds for his eyes to adjust to his darker surroundings. He nodded to the policeman. "Hello, Roy," Jimmy said.

"Jimmy," the officer answered.

"Chief, I was in town to get some harness leather, and I thought maybe you'd let me walk rounds with you again."

"Sure, Jimmy. I was just about to go out." Bull rose from his chair.

"Great, Chief, thanks," Jimmy said.

"Leave your sidearm here."

Jimmy's smile weakened a little, but he replied, "All right," and he unbuckled his gun belt and hung it on a peg on the wall.

Bull had been anticipating the disappointment on the young man's face, and, though it mattered little to him, he nevertheless had a ready cure for it. He wanted Jimmy to understand that law enforcement was not play, and he thought he could make the point. He opened his desk drawer and picked out an auxiliary badge.

"We might as well make this official, Jimmy. Come over here."

Jimmy's eyes lit up, and he walked around the desk to the police chief.

"Raise your right hand, son."

Jimmy did as he was told, his face serious in keeping with the moment.

"Do you promise to uphold the law?"

"Yes, sir!" Jimmy blurted. Then he added, "I mean, I do."

Without changing expression, Bull pinned the badge on

Jimmy's shirt. The policeman, watching Jimmy trying to hide his enthusiasm, had to turn away to hide his own amusement. Jimmy looked down at the badge and was tempted to shine it with his shirtsleeve but thought that would look a little too childish. He looked up, took a deep breath, and squared his shoulders. He was ready.

Jimmy was twenty-two, not really a boy anymore. He was the son of a farmer and still worked the farm and raised horses on the side. He could be all business when it came to his horses and their care and breeding, but when it came to his dream of being a lawman, he had a childish eagerness that belied his age.

"Roy, take care of the office until we get back. Then you can go home, and I'll do rounds tonight."

"Mighty fine, Chief." The policeman settled into the chair that Bull had just risen from.

Bull buckled on his own gun belt and motioned for Jimmy to precede him into the street. Jimmy rubbed his palms on his pants, opened the door, and stepped into the afternoon sunlight.

Fort Wayne was a quiet town in the middle of farmland. It had no need of an extensive police force or sheriff's depart-ment. Roy, the policeman, only worked a few hours a week; Chief Bull Johannsen was able to keep the peace in all but the most extraordinary circumstances. That afternoon was to be one of those circumstances.

"Let's drop in at the café, Jimmy."

"Right," Jimmy said.

All was peaceful at the café. The chief chatted briefly with a few early diners while Jimmy stood stiffly and a little apart out of respect for what he assumed were personal conversations. The chief, seemingly casual, was watching Jimmy closely. The young man sometimes seemed to be a little excitable, and he didn't want his presence to be the cause of an incident. He forced himself to admit that, with the right guidance, Jimmy might eventually become a good peace officer. They left the café in silence.

Jimmy tried to keep pace with the chief without seeming to walk in step, while his eyes scanned everything taking place within his view. This, he had read, was what a good lawman should do. He glanced quickly down at his badge and then brought his eyes up to the street once more.

"Tavern," the chief said, and he nodded in the direction of JB's Tavern, a little bar on a side street. Jimmy walked toward it alongside him.

"You been in a saloon before, son?"

"Yeah . . . well, I guess . . . not really . . . I guess." Jimmy didn't want to lie on the first day he wore a badge.

"Don't get distracted by the women. They probably won't be dressed the way your mother dresses."

"Yes, sir."

"When we first walk in, watch the bartender; he'll let you know if something is wrong by his expression."

"Yes, sir."

In front of the tavern were two soldiers in uniform. The chief paused as one of them held up a hand.

The soldier spoke. "There's a real ugly card game going on in there, Officer," the soldier warned.

"Did you lose some money?" Bull asked.

"Only had to play one hand to see the cards coming from the bottom," he answered. "I folded. Don't need the trouble." He tapped the stripes on his sleeve.

"All right, thanks, Sarge." Bull patted the soldier on the arm. The two men left, and Bull and Jimmy entered the tavern.

The inside was dark, cool, and smoky. Bull and Jimmy let their eyes adjust, and then they saw a table with seven men playing cards. One man was raking a large pot to himself, smiling. No one else was. There was a tension in the room that even Jimmy could feel. He looked at the bartender to see if he would tip them off, but the bar was crowded, and the bartender seemed oblivious to the events at the table. When Jimmy looked back, Bull had moved around behind the winner as another hand was being dealt. Jimmy decided the best place for him was on the opposite side of the table. He stepped in behind a man who was scowling. Jimmy watched the man who had won the last hand pick up the cards he was being dealt. The scowling man, Carlson, spoke.

"You ain't gonna win this hand, Mac," he said as he picked up his own cards.

"We'll see," the recent winner replied.

A man sitting next to Carlson said, under his breath but loudly enough to be heard by everyone at the table, "It's a lot harder for 'im when he don't deal."

The recent winner replied, "The way you play, if you don't like losing, you shouldn't sit down." He smiled at his own joke.

"Open for two bits," said a player.

Jimmy could see that Carlson had picked up three jacks. He then picked up a queen and another. But his opportunity to get revenge on the winner was not to be. The winner threw in his cards.

"I'm out," he said, still smiling.

"You cheatin' son of a coyote!" the disappointed Carlson said loudly.

The winner, not willing to let another insult go unanswered, produced a pistol from under his vest and cocked it. Bull was ready. He reached over the man's shoulder and grabbed his gun hand, putting his thumb under the hammer so it couldn't fall.

Carlson, undeterred by Bull's interference, got up from his chair and looked as if he were going to climb over the table and attack the winner, gun or no gun.

Jimmy grabbed Carlson's shoulders from behind and pressed him back into his chair. Carlson swung blindly back at Jimmy and hit him hard in the stomach. Jimmy lost his grip on the man's shoulders.

Across the table another player entered the fight and pulled Bull down, freeing the man with the gun. This man had been an accomplice to the winner's cheating, and they both had considerable winnings that they stood to lose in this confrontation. They were professionals who had dealt with this type of situation many times in the past. This wouldn't be the first game they had been thrown out of. They both knew that they had to maintain control, or they could lose everything.

Carlson now drew his belt knife and again moved to cross

the table and exact the revenge that he was unable to attain with cards. Bull was getting up from the floor as the two gamblers on his side of the table, one of them with the gun still in his hand, made ready to deal with the man with the knife. There were also several sympathetic card players ready to back Carlson, in spite of the gambler with the gun. One of these players picked up a chair. Violence was taking over the room. Behind Jimmy, the bartender, crouching low behind the bar, was leveling a shotgun at the entire group around the table. Patrons not involved with the card game were edging toward the door, keeping their eyes on the brawl. Bloodshed seemed inevitable.

Jimmy had broad shoulders and powerful arms, the product of shoeing horses from the age of ten. He wrapped his right arm tightly around the throat of the man with the knife, who swung backward again but was unable to make solid contact this time. Using his and Carlson's combined weight to brace himself, Jimmy put his left foot against the card table and sent it crashing into the two gamblers just as the one with the gun was ready to pull the trigger. The gun discharged into the ceiling and fell to the floor; the two men were sent reeling backward, along with Bull and several other men. Jimmy threw Carlson powerfully to the floor, leaving him there. Then he flipped the table out of his way and, moving forward quickly, scooped the gambler's revolver off the floor. He lowered the hammer, not wanting to take a chance on an accidental discharge, but kept his thumb on it. By this time Bull had regained his feet and had his own revolver drawn.

"Hold it!" he bellowed. "Everyone, stay right where you

are!" He pointed his revolver at each man in turn to reinforce his order.

Jimmy watched as the men complied.

The bartender lowered his shotgun.

Fifteen minutes later four men were in jail and the winnings had been confiscated, as had the gambler's revolver and the other man's knife. Bull, Roy, and Jimmy were sitting in the police station, drinking coffee.

"You shoulda' been there, Roy. Best brawl we've had in a coupla years."

"I guess I'll leave that kind of stuff to you, Bull," Roy replied. "I get all the excitement I need just writing tickets."

"Well, I'm glad we don't have to do that kind of thing often, but it's good to know a man can still deal with it if he has to."

"Hard to believe no one got killed," Roy added.

"Yeah." Bull turned to Jimmy. "How about you, young man? How do you like law enforcement work now?"

"Oh . . . well . . . I think things happen a little faster than when you're behind a plow."

The other two men broke out into friendly laughter, and Jimmy joined in.

Chapter Three

Marshal "Brink" Bringham was still laughing as he entered his office in Cheyenne. The barber from whom he had just come always had a new, funny story to tell, and he knew how to tell them. Brink ran a hand around the back of his neck and thought to himself that the barber was good at two things; many men weren't, in his opinion. He was still smiling as he opened the morning's mail.

The mail contained WANTED flyers, court documents, requests for information, a letter from someone named Whipwell in Indiana, and, more pleasantly, a letter from his daughter in New York.

He hadn't seen his daughter in six years, but that was soon to change. In the letter she informed him she would be coming to Cheyenne in June. Coming home. Did she consider Wyoming home now? She had been in New York for almost as much time as she had lived with him in Cheyenne. He could find no mention of how long she might stay. They had kept in touch by letter over the years, made easier recently by the mail service provided by the railroad. Although the transcontinental railroad had not been completed until 1869, Cheyenne had been on the rail since 1867.

The letter was also full of news about people he had never met, places he had never been, and social events that he could not even imagine. He always read every word, not to learn more about those things but to see and appreciate how she put words together to try to bring those people and places to him. It was almost like hearing the sound of her voice and seeing the expressions on her face. He had saved all her letters for six years, and, when he had the time, he liked to retrieve her earlier missives from the bottom drawer of his desk and compare them to her more recent ones. Then he would lean back in his chair and close his eyes to conjure up her image and try to imagine how she was growing, maturing.

Her last few paragraphs in each letter inevitably expressed her deepest feelings about current events, her politics, and her faith. These he liked the best. After reading and rereading the letter several times, he reluctantly put it aside to get on with business.

With the exception of the letter from Indiana, the rest of the mail looked routine, so he opened the Whipwell letter next.

It could be from some old friend that he knew in the war, or perhaps an inquiry from another marshal or police chief.

Sometimes he received requests for information on the price of land or the availability of services in this mysterious land west of the Mississippi. It was easy for any curious person to draft a question or two and then slip the note into an envelope addressed only to a nonspecific marshal or mayor or town council. With the railway service extending all the way to New York City, and mail traveling as fast as iron wheels on a steel rail, Marshal Bringham received more than a few of these.

Brink read the letter and laid it on the desk while he poured himself a cup of coffee. Then he picked it up and read it again. It seemed straightforward enough, but something about it was puzzling to him, and he couldn't put his finger on it. The letter was from a twenty-two-year-old man in Indiana looking for work as a peace officer, and it seemed to offer a solution to a problem that Brink shared with his employer, the town of Cheyenne.

Since the coming of the railroad over three years ago, Cheyenne was booming. There were opportunities and work for anyone who was willing, and that posed difficulties for him. In his experience, when money started flowing, crime and violence soon followed, and he already had more than he could do. To make matters worse, good deputies were soon lured away by better situations involving less danger and more money, and Brink had lost two men to other jobs since the first of the year. This young man with the unusual last name might provide a solution, at least until the trail drives were over in the fall.

Maybe what was bothering Brink was that Whipwell listed so many references, all seemingly respectable. Or maybe it was that the man's penmanship and language were both good. Would a well-educated man be adaptable to the rough-and-tumble streets of Cheyenne? And how did such a young man get four years experience as a marshal in the town of Marion? No, although those things seemed a little odd, what really bothered him was the writer's bold statement that he was better with handguns than anyone he knew. In Brink's experience, men who were proficient with weapons seldom bragged about it.

Before the war Brink had met the police chief in Fort Wayne, the nearest town of consequence, but he had no idea if the man had survived the war, much less was still the chief. Brink considered writing to the town of Fort Wayne to try to find out what kind of marshal the young man had been and to determine the fate of an old acquaintance. He took a sheet of writing paper from his desk, but instead of writing to Fort Wayne, he wrote a reply directly to the young man.

April 4, 1870
Dear Mr. Whipwell:

Your letter was given to me by the mayor of Cheyenne. As it happens, we have recently decided that the town of Cheyenne needs another deputy marshal. However, I can't promise you a job without meeting you in person. If you could come to Cheyenne before the first of July, we could talk this over. I can hold the job open until

then. Let me know by telegram if you are willing to travel to Cheyenne on chance.
Best Regards,
Harold Bringham
Marshal, City of Cheyenne, Wyoming

Brink addressed an envelope, folded and inserted the letter, and sealed the flap. He had plenty of time; the eastbound train wouldn't be in until the next morning. He looked at the other envelopes and selected one from the Omaha Police Department. In it he found a WANTED poster, a well-done drawing of a man wanted for embezzlement of bank funds and assault.

Most pictures on WANTED posters were not well done, and Brink seldom spent much time studying them. But this embezzler's picture was very lifelike; the artist must have known the man to have put so much feeling into his portrait. The picture was of a man who wore his hair to his collar and was clean shaven, but what particularly fascinated Brink was the difference between the man's eyes. Brink used the envelope to cover the left half of the man's face. The man looked intelligent and congenial. When he covered the right half of the man's face in the same way, the face took on a malevolent, menacing look. It was like looking at two different men. Brink tacked the poster to the wall above his desk and looked at it as if he were waiting for the likeness to blink. Finally he rubbed his eyes and turned away. It was time to walk through the downtown district, to see and be seen. He put the remainder of the week's mail into a tray and pushed his chair back from the desk.

Before Brink opened the office door to walk out into the street, he smoothed the legs of his pants, touched his badge, lifted his revolver from its holster, let it settle back gently into the leather, and put on his hat. He was so familiar with his revolver that he could determine whether or not it was loaded just by the weight in his hand. He stepped into the street and shaded his eyes from the late-afternoon sun with his left hand. His right hand was always near the Colt's 1860 Army.

Chapter Four

Nate Jackson waited until dark to slip into Omaha's back streets to find his brother. He probably wouldn't be recognized, even by his former friends, but he didn't want to take any chances. A month ago he had been clean shaven with moderately long hair. Now he had a full beard and carefully shaved his head every few days, seldom wearing a hat, so that this feature would be prominent. His hands were callused from his employment as a deckhand on a riverboat. He also wore glasses, which were quite weak. The glasses disturbed his vision, but he felt they were worth it. In his weeks of living the life of a fugitive, his skin had darkened and he had lost weight, and that completed his metamorphosis.

He would be done with that life soon. The information he had stolen from the bank dictated that he come back to Omaha and recruit help for a bigger payoff than the fruitless bank robbery ever could have supplied.

The little cabin on the edge of town where Abraham Jackson lived was dark. Nate located it by moonlight and, after making sure no one was on the street, stepped out of the shadows and up to the door, where he tapped three times. The door opened, and he quickly entered.

In the light from the one lamp in the room, Abe looked at his brother and said, "Dang, man, you look like a hard chance. You been eatin'?"

"I'm doing all right. Where's Penny?" Penny was a dancer who lived with Abraham Jackson.

"She's working at the Cattleman's. Prob'ly be after midnight before she comes home."

"Good," Nate declared. "She doesn't need to know that I'm in town."

Abe fetched some biscuits and a bottle of whiskey from the cupboard, and the two men sat down at the table. Nate took a biscuit and ate it quickly, then another, and then swigged a long drink from the bottle as Abe watched. Abe had never seen his brother drink straight liquor before.

Finally Nate asked, "Has anyone been around looking for me?"

"Oh, yeah. A policeman came and told me to tell you to give yourself up if I saw you, and a detective the bank hired came and asked me some questions."

"What kind of questions? Is this all you've got to eat?"

"I got a can of beans." Abe got up to get the beans. "He

asked me if I'd seen you since the robbery and if we'd talked about it before you did it. Shoot, I didn't tell him anything, just played dumb."

"That's all?"

"He said if the bank didn't get the money back, they'd take your house away from your wife and kid and put 'em on the street."

Nate had no comment. He doubted that the bank would do this, but he didn't particularly care. He had played the role of a family man in the years since the war, but he had become tired of it and wanted more from life than he was likely to achieve in Omaha. And, although his wife was a decent, faithful woman, she no longer interested him.

Marriage had seemed like a sensible thing to do, and his wife had seemed like a sensible person to marry, but ten years of providing for her and a child, and then another to come, reporting to work every day and toiling at a job he found stifling, had chipped away at the façade of civility with which he had covered himself. When he struck down the banker's nephew, he had found no regret, but rather felt as though he had been swimming underwater for years, holding his breath beyond what was possible and then suddenly breaking the surface for his first deep gulp of air. He would never swim underwater again, nor report to the bank, nor wait for a meager paycheck at month's end.

"And one other thing, Nate."

"What?"

"The kid, Stephen Hopkins, died last week."

"What killed him?"

Abe watched his brother's face closely as he answered, "You did."

"That makes no sense. I only hit him." He remembered striking the man and kicking him; surely those blows could not have brought about death. "He was swearing at me when I left."

"Maybe so, but he started having fits, and the doc couldn't do anything. I heard they went on for a couple of days, gettin' worse all the time, until he just quit breathin'."

"And they're blaming me for that?"

"Yeah," was all Abe could say.

Nate felt a cold fear that he controlled with difficulty. He was flirting with a hangman's noose now. He briefly considered jumping up and running from the cabin, from the town, getting as far away as possible before he was discovered. He suddenly felt he could trust no one, not even his own brother, for there would surely be a substantial reward offered for his capture. He suppressed the fear and let logic take over. No matter his status with the law, he could make it no worse now; what he needed was money to finance a complete getaway, and he had a plan that would gain him that. This was where he needed Abe.

"Did you find some men to help us?" he asked, trying to keep his voice normal.

"Yeah, them Hollister brothers, Eddie and Bump. They just come into town." Abe poured some beans from a pot on the stove into a bowl and set it and a spoon in front of his brother.

"I remember them. They were in my regiment. They're both tough characters and not stupid. Can we trust them?"

Abe hesitated a moment before answering. He had been involved with the Hollisters in several questionable escapades. "Yeah, 'til we have somethin' they want. Then we better be ready to deal with 'em."

"All right, we'll be ready," was all Nate had to say to this. He continued eating quietly but earnestly.

Abe squirmed in his seat. He started to say something several times, eventually found his courage, and asked his brother, "Nate, how's about letting me have some money, like an advance?" Nate scowled at his brother, who quickly added, "I just need to get a few things for Penny. She's been feedin' me all winter."

Nate put his spoon into the now empty bowl. "I didn't get any gold when I stole that Wells Fargo box." He wiped his mouth on his sleeve.

His brother was surprised. "You had to! I mean, why did you . . . I mean, you were supposed to . . ."

Nate interrupted Abe. "Yeah, I was supposed to get five thousand dollars worth of gold, but there was no gold in the box."

"Well, dang, man. Why did you steal it if it didn't have no gold?"

Nate had difficulty controlling his impulse to hit his brother in the face. It was bad enough that he had thrown his life away for very little profit; it made him furious to be reminded.

"Hopkins came in just as I was opening the safe. I had to take care of him, and then it was too late to back out. I could tell the box was too light, but there was nothing else in the safe, so I took the box and left. When I broke it open, I found about four hundred dollars in cash. No gold."

"That ain't hardly enough to set up this next job, is it?"

"It'll have to be. I also have my savings that I had the forethought to withdraw before. I take it you have no money to spare?"

"Shoot, I ain't got no money at all. Penny'll come home with four or five dollars, but we'll use that for grub."

Nate was irritated at his brother, but he kept silent. For all his schemes, Abraham never seemed to be able to take care of himself, much less contribute his share. But Nate, because of his fugitive status, was dependent on his brother at this time and would be forced to depend on him, in spite of his misgivings.

Abe spoke. "You want me to arrange a sit-down with the Hollisters?"

"Yeah, try to get 'em here tomorrow night. But don't tell them anything about the bank job. They could use that to force us to give them a bigger share or even turn me in for a quick payoff."

Abe's eyebrows went up; the comment surprised him. This more devious side of his brother was relatively strange to him. It made perfect sense to him to keep the two shady characters in the dark, but Nate had always been the trusting, good boy, while Abe had been the troublemaker. Nate was the son who did his chores without being told, learned his lessons in school, was always where he was supposed to be. Abe had always looked for a way to get out of whatever responsibility had fallen on him, always sought to gain an advantage over anyone he dealt with. *Anyone.* It seemed that his brother had suddenly converted to the kind of lifestyle with which he himself was more familiar. Abe had looked up to his older brother while they were growing up, and Nate's present way of life stood in stark contrast to his idealized memories.

"And find some way to get Penny out of the cabin. We don't need the whole world knowing what we're going to do."

"Yeah, all right."

"I've got a cold camp about a mile from here in the river bottom. I'll take the rest of those biscuits. Don't tell Penny anything. Don't tell the Hollisters anything—just get 'em here. I'll tell them all they need to know." Nate got up and buttoned his coat.

Maybe it was Nate's newly bald head, but Abe thought he looked taller and tougher than he had only a few months ago.

"Look around outside and see if anyone is on the street."

Abe did as he was told. In seconds his brother was gone and had disappeared into the shadows of the alley, while Abe, the scalawag brother, sat down at his table in his warm cabin and poured himself a drink.

Chapter Five

Jonas Whipwell was a hardworking, honest, Indiana farmer who had built up a large farm with help from his wife and two older sons, Richard and Ronald. He was stern but not cruel, considered himself to be ordinary, was intolerant of fools, and, although he occasionally had self-doubts, he was outwardly self-assured and confident. As a Christian, he always tried to avoid harming others, but people who knew him tended to stay out of his path. His single-minded work ethic had brought him much success in agriculture, and at this time of his life he could have relaxed and let his two older sons run his farm, but that was not his nature. He still oversaw and took satisfaction in every detail of the business.

His third son, James, had come along much later and become his mother's favorite. When Richard and Ronald were hard at work in the fields, James was either in school or with his mother in the house studying, while she handled the household chores and gardening. James was bright, energetic, and more than capable of being helpful, even while quite young, but she wanted him to get the knowledge and culture for which her two older boys could not afford to take the time.

She—Olivia was her name—had wanted a girl but was happy to get another child of either sex, as long as he or she was a companion and, eventually a confidant in her male-dominated world. For his part, Jimmy adored his mother and did anything and everything to please her and, because of her support, was often excused from the more unpleasant work on the expanding family farm. His role was similar to that of an only child because of the age difference between himself and his two older brothers.

Jimmy's main contribution to the farm was raising horses—a joint effort between him and his mother—almost from the time he could walk. His father thought little of the enterprise but tolerated it, partly because of the love he had for Olivia and partly because it got Jimmy out of the house. The schooling that Jimmy received from his mother in literature, art, and geography was of little value as far as Jonas Whipwell was concerned.

When the Civil Was started, Jimmy was only thirteen. His brothers were excused from serving as they were needed to work the farm, which provided food and other supplies for the war effort. Eager to be on his own, Jimmy enlisted in the final year of the war, joining a cavalry unit, where his knowledge of horses would be useful.

But the war ended, Jimmy's regiment was disbanded, and

he was discharged after barely learning to use a pistol. The seeds were sown, however; he became fascinated with firearms and purchased a succession of pistols with which he strove to become proficient. He was already competent at handling and riding horses and so found himself intrigued with stories of the far West, an area of the country that seemed entirely dependent on horses and guns. This led to his involvement with the police chief of Fort Wayne and eventually to his writing to over a dozen small towns in the West, looking for work as a deputy. With his knowledge of guns and his skill with horses, he fancied himself the equivalent of a frontiersman and wanted to leave the dull life of farming behind.

Another factor in his restlessness was the desire to escape his father. His mother had died the year following his return from the Army, and the next four years were a time of frequent conflict with his father and brothers. His only success in agriculture was his horse breeding, and he managed to produce profit with little assistance from his family. They grudgingly admired his ability as a breeder, but they all felt that the farm would be more successful if he were to apply himself as they did and, by the way, sell off the horses.

An incident early in 1870 firmed Jimmy's resolve to find broader horizons. It was spring, and his two brothers were working in the fields. Jimmy was working in the corral where he kept his horses when his father found him.

"James," Jonas Whipwell said, "the harness on the big plow is coming apart. That's your job—take care of it."

Jimmy had been shoeing a horse and was at a point where he couldn't stop. As he struggled with the horse, Jimmy was forced to reply without making eye contact, even though he knew that that would increase his father's displeasure.

"I sold this horse yesterday. Tom Brown will be here today to take her home."

"You either take care of your work or I'll sell all the horses. Tom Brown isn't going to do our plowing."

"I put together a spare harness last week." The shoe was done. Jimmy released the horse and straightened up to face his father. "I'll take it out to the field and change them out. I can repair the old one tonight."

Jonas knew nothing of the extra harness, and this was the kind of initiative that he respected, but he couldn't let go of his anger. The two men stood facing each other, each waiting for the other to say something.

The father spoke first. "This is a farm, James, not a horse ranch."

And before Jimmy could reply, Jonas Whipwell turned and stalked back to the main house. Jimmy put the mare into a small corral near the road and picked up his tools.

The time had come.

When the letter from the marshal in Cheyenne arrived, Jimmy was excited but said nothing to his family, instead inquiring in Fort Wayne about fares and livestock shipping on the railroad west. When his plans were firm, he mustered his courage and sought out his father. He had spent the day repairing corrals—not the ones in which he kept his horses; they were always in good repair. The ones for the farm animals often suffered from neglect in the spring when there was so much other work to be done, and this was work that the farm needed and at which he was skilled.

He paused at the door to his father's study, took a deep breath, and walked in without knocking. His father didn't look up; he recognized the different sound that Jimmy's riding boots made on the hardwood floor. Without thinking about it, he usually made the determination each time Jimmy approached him that their meeting was not likely to profit him. It was usually about Jimmy's wanting something: more space in the barn, help in castrating or branding, or an advance on his anticipated profits for some kind of equipment that he suddenly found necessary. And there you had it; Jimmy contributed to the overall income of the farm without being given credit, and the family assisted him frequently with his endeavors without thanks.

"Father." Jimmy addressed his father, who continued writing without looking up. Jimmy waited, knowing it would not enhance the conversation were he to repeat his terse greeting. His father appreciated patience and demanded it from his family.

Jonas Whipwell looked up from his desk with his pencil in his hand as if he doubted that there would be any exchange between them that warranted a complete interruption of what he was doing. Jimmy played the game too. He knew not to avert his eyes but instead looked intently at his father and waited, just as his father had waited. When the senior Whipwell finally put the pencil down on the desk, Jimmy put his hands into his back pockets.

"Father, I'm leaving the farm," Jimmy said. His father's

expression didn't change. Jimmy repeated, "I'm leaving your house."

After a moment Jonas Whipwell answered, "When?"

His father was always right to the point. The one-word question indicated how little he wanted his son to think he cared about what he did, where he was going, why, or even how. But the fact was that he did care, and he very much wanted to know where and how. The why was easier to understand.

There was a lot Jimmy wanted to say that would explain why he was leaving, where he was going, and much, much, more, but he chose to be as brief as his father and answer only the immediate question. He would let his father open further discussion if he wished.

"Saturday, a week."

Jonas Whipwell studied his son's face to see if there was any hint of sorrow or regret. He could read his other sons' faces like open books; they were both like him, honest and open, if slightly less intelligent. James, he knew, was smarter, and he always thought Jimmy was honest, but he could never be sure; they simply weren't in tune with each other. He had never caught him in a lie, but he couldn't read his youngest son's face, just as he had not been able to read his wife's face when she was alive, and that caused him to be even more reserved with Jimmy than with other people.

It began to sink in that his youngest son, the son with so little ability to take care of himself or produce anything worthwhile, the son who reminded him daily of his beloved wife, was leaving—leaving shelter, leaving family, leaving

his hometown and his home state. It would have been difficult to understand if it had been either of the older sons; it
bordered on incredible that it was Jimmy. He had always
thought that all his sons, especially James, would stay on the
farm forever.

"What about your horses?"

"I want to take the two big stallions, the old gelding, and
six of the best mares, if that's acceptable." The gelding was
Jimmy's sentimental favorite, he was gentle and easy to ride,
and he had a calming effect on the rest of the horses. "The
rest I'll leave for you." Then Jimmy added, "They're all
good horses, and they're worth a lot of money."

"Yes, they are," Jonas acknowledged—high praise, coming from him. But then he added, "I should know. I'm the
one who's fed them for years." He was immediately sorry he
had said that, but he kept his face expressionless. As a matter
of fact, the horses had always been profitable for the farm,
but he wanted *all* his sons to be farmers. Horses bred for riding were frivolous, in his opinion.

Jimmy ignored both the praise and the complaint. "I'm
going to string them to Fort Wayne and take them with me
on the train west. I have applied for a job as deputy marshal
at Cheyenne, and I just received a reply from the marshal
there." He didn't elaborate that it was only for an interview.
If his father had been about to ask what the reply contained,
he didn't get the chance. James went on. "I'm going to breed
horses out there also, and I need my best stallions and mares.
There's a good market for horses with the Army."

"I understand horses run wild out there."

"Yes, in some places, but my horses are of much higher quality." Jimmy stood ever so slightly straighter as he said that.

It might have been that the old man appreciated that his youngest son was taking on a huge challenge that he himself might have taken when he was younger. Or it might have been that, in spite of all the conflict between them, he still had real affection for the "runt of the litter," as he had called him in earlier years. For whatever reason, Jonas Whipwell did something then that astounded his son. He arose, walked slowly around his desk, and took Jimmy's right hand in his, holding Jimmy's elbow with his left hand, not shaking it or squeezing it, just holding it. Then he shook it just once and released it as he looked into his son's eyes. For just a moment it was Olivia looking back at him, and he had to take a deep breath.

Jimmy met his father's gaze without blinking, surprised at the intimacy of the moment but suddenly more confident in his father's presence than he had ever been before. He looked into his father's eyes, knowing that his father was about to speak but not having any idea what he would say. Would he tell Jimmy that it was high time he left, as he had never pulled his weight? Would he say what most parents say in these situations—"You're always welcome to come back home?" Not likely, Jimmy thought.

"You're leaving the farm forever, I know, and you're leaving the family you've lived with all your life. But you can't leave the Whipwell name," Jonas Whipwell said. Then he added after a long pause, "Do it honor."

For the first time in his life, Jimmy began to see his father for the man he truly was. He was tempted to say much, much more, but instead replied, "I will, Father. I will."

Jonas Whipwell returned to his chair behind his desk, sat down, looked up once at his son, who was still standing in the same spot, and then picked up his pencil and began writing again. Jimmy looked down at the floor, then back at his father, and turned and walked out of the room.

Chapter Six

Marshal Bringham stepped from his office into the cool evening air of May in Wyoming. The sounds of the evening came to him from all sides, and his mind sorted them, labeled them, and filed them. There was a piano playing from somewhere on Main Street, normal on a Saturday, and laughter from several locations, also normal. As he passed the café, he could hear dishes clinking and low conversation. He looked in the window of the door to see how many people he recognized.

The Army's first patrols of their spring campaigns against the Sioux had returned; suppliers of farm equipment and seed had their salesmen in the field to take advantage of spring planting; Cheyenne was a hub for a steady stream of immigrants traveling the wagon roads. At this time of year he knew he was likely not to know everyone in the room, and he was correct. There was an officer from the fort eating with the station manager for the Union Pacific; there was one of the local ranchers dining with his foreman and a cowboy; there were four cowboys from another ranch supping together. The other people Brink also knew except for a salesman he didn't recognize, but he recognized the type; he just couldn't guess what the man might be selling. He knew he would eventually find out.

Next, he passed the barbershop, which was closed, then the pharmacy, Foster's General Store, and a boot shop, all closed. That put him at the corner and standing in front of the bat-wing doors of the Main Street Saloon. As he was standing there, the bartender came to close the main doors in order to preserve the afternoon's warmth.

"You coming in, Marshal?" the bartender asked politely, not wanting to close the doors in Brink's face.

Brink leaned over the bat wings and surveyed the room while the bartender waited. "No, I guess not, Sam. Do you have any trouble brewing in there?"

"Too early. Give it a few more hours." He smiled good-naturedly at the marshal.

"I 'spect so, Sam." He grinned back. "Well, I'll be back later, or else Bob will if I'm busy. See ya."

"Sure thing, Marshal." Sam slowly closed the doors, watching the marshal as he did so to ensure that the lawman had seen everything he might want to see.

Brink crossed the street diagonally to look in on another saloon, actually a dance hall, where women were hired to dance and drink with patrons. This was the place that usually generated the problems, and tonight it would likely follow its all too familiar pattern.

As Brink stepped up onto the boardwalk at the Frontier Dance Hall, he noticed that one of the lamps on the outside of the building was not burning. He made a mental note to tell the bartender about it. Brink liked to have the boardwalks along Main Street lit until at least midnight.

The main doors had not yet been closed against the cool of the evening, and Brink looked into the lighted room to size it up before entering. The bartender was behind the bar, polishing glasses. There were several couples dancing—awkward young cowboys with older women heavily made up. Two card games were under way with a few kibitzers.

Pretty quiet for a Saturday night. Maybe I'll get to bed early tonight.

Brink stepped through the bat-wing doors and walked to the bar as he continued to survey the room. He walked behind the bar to stand with the bartender, still watching the room.

The bartender looked up from his work as Brink approached him. "Marshal," he greeted Brink.

"Hi, Slim," Brink replied. "You've got everything under control tonight, it looks like."

"Yeah, I guess the ranches kept their men out of town tonight. There's lots of work to do this time of year and not enough men to do it."

"Can't say I'm sorry, but I know it's not good for business."

Brink leaned on the bar and continued to watch the room

as they chatted about the weather, the coming summer, the railroad, and Indians. Brink changed the subject as he focused on one of the card games. There were four men seated around a table and a bar girl standing behind one of them, a middle-aged man in range clothes.

"Who's the redhead behind the cowman?" Brink asked in a low voice.

"That's April. She came to town this week, and I put her to work. She's young, but she seems to know what she's doing."

"Yeah, she does. She's tipping the cowman's hand to someone else at the table. Watch her fingers."

Slim swore quietly and watched as the cowman folded, and the game went on without him until another player raked in the pot. During the next hand, a well-dressed man seated opposite the cowman folded, and April looked around the room as if bored.

Brink and Slim continued to discuss various subjects as they waited for another hand to be dealt.

This time the cowman and the well-dressed man stayed in while the other two men folded. Slim and Brink watched April's hands on the shoulders of the cowman. There was no doubt she was signaling the well-dressed man across from him.

Brink stood up straight.

Slim said, "I'll take care of it if you want." Slim knew it was important to show that his bar was intolerant of cheaters.

"Go ahead, Slim. I'll back you."

Slim pulled a wooden club from under the bar and walked around the end into the room. Brink walked around the other end. Slim walked up to the right of the gambler and slapped the stick into his other hand, saying, "Pick up your chips and cash in, Mister. You're done in here."

"What are you talking about? I'm just playing cards!" the man protested.

"I said you're done. Pick up, cash in, and get out!" Slim emphasized.

The other three men looked surprised. The gambler reached under his coat with his right hand, and Brink stepped up and grabbed the man's hand as it closed on a small pistol. Brink was strong, and his grip crushed the man's fingers against the firearm, causing him to swear. The man struggled to get out of his chair and stand.

"Just relax, Mister," Brink advised. The man didn't relax; he got his feet under himself and tried to get up, but he couldn't free his right hand from Brink's grasp. As he half stood, he swung his left fist hard into Brink's stomach. Brink grunted but didn't relax his grip. Instead, he kicked the man's legs out from under him, and the gambler went down. This allowed the man to wrench his right hand from Brink, and he pulled the pistol from his belt. Just as it seemed that he might gain the advantage and do real harm, Slim's club slammed into the man's arm, and the pistol went flying. Brink grabbed the man's left arm and rolled him roughly onto his stomach as the man cried in pain. In seconds he was in handcuffs and no longer a threat.

Brink gave Slim a look of gratitude and then directed his attention to the bar girl, April. Her eyes were wide, and she looked scared. "Your name's April, right?" he asked.

"Y-y-yes," she answered with a tremulous voice.

"Where are you staying?"

"Upstairs."

"You follow me to the jail. Don't you dare try to run, understand?"

The girl nodded.

Brink had one more thing to say to the other three at the card table before he took the gambler and April away. "I'm confiscating this man's winnings. After his fine and court costs are paid, you three can split up what's left. Any problem with that?" He looked at the three men who had been playing with the cheater. They all shook their heads to indicate no. Brink had already scooped up the man's chips and handed them to Slim. "I'll be back for the cash later, Slim."

"All right, Marshal. Anything else?"

"Yeah, come to think of it. You've got a lamp out on the west side."

"I'll get it taken care of, no problem."

April fell in obediently behind Brink as he pushed the gambler ahead toward the door, her heart in her throat. She had never been locked up in a jail before.

At the door to the jail, Brink unlocked it and pushed it open, and then told April, "Go on in and light the lamp." She did as she was told; by now her stomach was in knots, and she thought she might throw up.

She'll do anything a man asks her to do. That's what got her into this mess.

When the lamp was lit, Brink pushed the gambler into the room as April watched. She might have run, but she knew she couldn't outrun the marshal in the shoes she was wearing. Brink locked the gambler in a cell and then held a gun on him as he made the gambler remove his own handcuffs and pass them and the key back through the bars. Then he had the man remove his coat and vest to make sure he had no other weapons. He took the garments and the man's pistol and locked them in the bottom drawer of his gun cabinet. At last he turned his attention to April.

"Come over here, April." She had both hands on her stomach, now sure of her fate.

"Take a good look at that cell." She did, and what she saw almost finished her stomach. She had to close her eyes and swallow twice before opening them to see what he wanted her to see. There was a thin, stained mattress on an iron shelf. No dresser, no mirror, no chair, and just a rusty bucket on the floor.

The marshal studied her face as she looked in horror at the cell. She was younger than he'd thought, probably about the same age as his daughter. Her nose was slightly off center, and one ear was disfigured where it might have been cut with a knife and healed crookedly.

"Have you seen enough?"

April looked at him in puzzled surprise. What was he going to do?

"Let's go," he said, and he started toward the door. She followed, still not sure what was going to happen to her. He waited at the door for her to exit and then followed, locking the door behind them.

As they approached the Frontier Dance Hall, Brink stopped at the bottom of the steps and turned to April.

"Your friend is going to be in jail for a while. He may end up in prison." He paused to watch her face. She said nothing. "You're under arrest too. I want you to go up to your room and stay there. I'll tell Slim, and I'll have food sent to you. Don't leave your room for any reason, and don't let anyone in, or I'll put you in that cell you just saw." Brink's voice was stern. "Understand?"

"Yes," she answered in a small voice. She had been holding her breath and still couldn't believe she was not going to jail.

Brink softened. "Look," he said, "I'm not going to run you out of town and let you be someone else's problem, and I doubt that the judge will put you in jail." She was standing on the first step so that they were at eye level with each other. "The café, the laundry, and the hotel are all looking for hired help. I'll talk to the judge Monday morning, and you'll probably be free Monday afternoon. Do yourself a favor. . . ." He didn't finish because he could tell she understood everything he was saying. He turned toward the door and motioned her to lead the way.

Inside the dance hall Brink explained to Slim what he was doing.

"She's not working for room and board anymore, Slim.

She's under arrest. The county will pay you for her room for the next two days, and I'll have food sent over for her."

"Whatever you say, Marshal."

"She's not to come downstairs until I come for her Monday."

Slim, having seen angry miners burn down a saloon they thought was cheating them, wanted the girl out of his establishment forever, but he reluctantly agreed to let her stay under house arrest through the weekend. Brink took the gambler's winnings, counted them in front of Slim, and returned to patrolling the streets of Cheyenne.

Chapter Seven

Once again Nate watched and listened from the shadows on the back street of Omaha where his brother lived. He didn't know from which direction the Hollisters would come, if they showed, but he wanted the chance to observe them before their meeting. After talking to his brother, he had formed the opinion that they were dangerous men who neither owed nor gave loyalty to anyone. Those qualities might be valuable for the purpose he had in mind, but the brothers would have to be watched closely. It was like buying snakes for self-protection.

The sound of footsteps in the mud of the street attracted Nate's attention. He pressed against the wall of a vacant building, blending with the shadows cast by a lighted window across the street. It was a woman carrying an earthen pot. She walked within fifteen feet of Nate without seeing him and continued down the street. As Nate watched her walk away, he could see two large forms walking toward her. *This must be Ed and Bump Hollister.* As they passed the woman, the larger man turned to follow her but was restrained by the other. Nate could barely see the woman in the darkness of the street, but he was sure she quickened her pace. He thought he could hear angry words between the two men, and then they returned to their route. This was consistent with what he knew about the Hollister brothers—mean, tough, and with little regard for others.

The two men stopped at the front door of Abraham's cabin and knocked loudly on it. This confirmed to Nate that they were indeed the Hollister brothers. The door opened, they entered, and the door closed. Nate looked both ways along the street and then walked quickly to Abe's front door, where he waited and listened. Nothing. Finally he knocked, and in a second he was also inside.

Ed and Bump Hollister had taken their coats off and were hanging them on pegs on the wall. They both looked Nate over carefully.

"You Nate?" Ed asked.

"Yeah," Nate replied. "Which one of you is Ed, and which one is Bump?"

"I'm Ed," Ed answered. "That's Bump." He pointed at his brother.

Ed Hollister was six feet tall and solidly built. His hair was long and brown, his beard long enough to cover the top of his collar, and both hair and beard were ragged. His eyes were deeply set and held no sign of humor or compassion.

His brother, Bump, was even bigger and stronger and in contrast was clean shaven. His hair was cut short and uncombed, giving him a comical appearance. He had a pleasant suggestion of a smile on his face.

The four men sat around the table. There were only two chairs; Bump sat on a barrel, and Nate sat on a wooden box.

Nate opened the conversation. "Gentlemen, I know how we can make a lot of money, but I want to get one thing straight right now. I'm not going to tell you exactly what we're going to do until it's necessary." He looked at each man before he went on. "This isn't going to be a bang-bang job. It'll take a week for us to get it done, and I don't want everyone sitting around thinking and talking about it." He looked at Ed's face, believing him to be the smarter of the two brothers, and then added, "If that doesn't work for you, let's have a drink and go home. We'll find someone else or just give it up."

"Are you crazy?" Ed asked. "We ain't gonna promise anything unless we know what's going on!"

Nate had a reply ready. "That will be your choice to make, of course, but I'll tell you now that the take will be about forty thousand dollars. Don't be too hasty." Nate Jackson was using all the charms he had acquired in his banking career.

Ed was incredulous. "Forty each?" He asked.

"Unfortunately, no." Nate smiled. "Forty total, and we split five ways." He added quickly, "I get two shares."

Bump spoke, leaning toward his brother. "How much will I get?" he asked.

Ed was already trying to work out the division in his head.

Partly to buy time and partly because he really wanted to know, he asked, "How do you know the exact amount?"

"I know. Let's leave it at that," Nate said. He hoped that they were unaware that he had just robbed the bank where he had been employed.

"I don't like it," Ed stated. "No plan, no way of knowing what we're in for. This don't smell good."

"I can tell you that there won't be any shoot-outs or hard riding to get away."

"Yeah?" Ed said.

"Yeah. If everyone does his part, we won't fire a shot," Nate added.

Ed Hollister's eyes narrowed. He understood force. He was suspicious of anyone who thought he could rob a fortune and not kill someone.

Nate Jackson had said all he wanted to say. He leaned back and waited for Ed Hollister to make a decision.

"It still don't smell good," Ed repeated.

Nate stood up. "All right, then. I understand. I'll find someone else. Let's all have a drink." He was bluffing. He knew he couldn't find someone else in time. He also felt sure that these two men would not likely let the matter rest here, that they could and would dog him or his brother to get a scent of the money. It was too big a score for them to walk away from. But he was just as sure that to relinquish any information or control at this point would put his plan and his very life in danger. Further, if he backed down, they would suspect that he didn't plan to share the take when it was all over. It also occurred to him, conversely, that if they backed down, that might indicate that they had plans to dispose of him once they knew the plan.

Abe had been scribbling on the table, and now he spoke, "Eight thousand apiece." They all looked at him. "Eight thousand dollars," he repeated.

Ed looked over at Bump and then at Nate. "That's a pretty good hit, all right."

"It'll be every bit of that," Nate said. He was thinking of other wealth and valuables that would undoubtedly also be on the transcontinental train.

Ed Hollister ground his teeth. It was a lot of money to walk away from. Finally he spoke. "If it's as good you say, it's hard to pass." Then his voice got low. "It'd better be as good as you say. . ." He didn't finish.

Nate's eyes narrowed, but he forced a smile, "It's good. It might even be better than that. If you two do your part, the plan'll work, and we'll all be rich."

His smile seemed frozen, and, indeed, it was a cold, cold smile. All his life he had followed the rules and obeyed the laws, but once he had deviated from that pattern, there was no rule that couldn't be broken, no law that bound him, and no life that had value except his and his younger brother's. He knew that this enterprise was hazardous and becoming more so every minute, but he was equally sure that he was up to it, that he was smarter, and therefore deadlier, than both of these Hollisters put together.

Ed looked at Bump again, who nodded. "We're in, then."

It's the nature of criminal endeavors that, if great profits are to be the result, they can seldom be accomplished alone, and that means dangerous men must trust dangerous men. If it were not so, few people and few fortunes would be safe.

The plan was not complicated. Nate and one of the Hollisters would ride to Cheyenne on the westbound train and select a spot somewhere near Cheyenne where it would be easy to stop the train the next week. He wasn't sure how he would stop it—that would depend on what he found along the way—but he had several ideas that, from his experience in the war, were sure to be effective. Once he decided on an effective method, he and his Hollister accomplice would acquire what they needed in Cheyenne with the rest of his stolen bank money and then make their way back along the tracks to the selected holdup site in time to meet the next week's train. Abe and the other Hollister would be on that train and ready to disarm the crew when the train was forced to stop.

But this was not what was discussed among the four men.

"I want one of you men to go with me to Salt Lake City on next week's train. How about you, Bump?" Nate asked. The man's immense strength would be advantageous.

"Yeah, all right," Bump answered.

"I'll give you some money to buy two tickets. For reasons of my own, I'd rather not be seen at the train station." He pulled some bills from his pocket.

"I don't get it," Ed Hollister said.

Nate ignored Ed while he finished his instructions to Bump. "No Pullman car, understand?" He handed the money to Bump.

Bump nodded.

Nate turned to Ed Hollister. "You and Abe will follow on the next week's train."

Ed repeated, "I still don't get it."

Nate again ignored Ed's expressed doubts.

"Abe, you get two tickets to Salt Lake City," Nate instructed his brother.

Of course, neither Abe nor Ed Hollister would be going to Salt Lake City. It was Nate's way not only of confusing their trail if somehow the law found them out, but also of confusing the Hollisters, of preserving any advantage over these two dangerous brothers. Abe Jackson and Ed Hollister would be getting off the train before it arrived in Cheyenne, a crippled train in the middle of the prairie.

Nate told the Hollisters that he and Bump would ride the train together to Salt Lake City, not to the actual destination of Cheyenne, but they would not appear to know each other. They would separately rent rooms in a hotel while they made preparations, and, when the time came, Nate would tell Bump what he had to do. Abe and Ed would follow on the next train with two horses. They would also appear not to know each other while on the train. By splitting the two men, Nate and Abe would have the advantage should the relationship between the two sets of brothers deteriorate. Nate and Abe would know the entire plan and could also make contingency plans based on that advantage. Nate did not even share with them the fact that they would be robbing the very train on which his brother and Ed Hollister rode.

"That's all you got?" Ed asked.

"That's it." Nate answered. He waited to see if Ed Hollister tried to renegotiate the split. If he did, that meant that, although he might not be satisfied with his assigned split, he intended to follow the plan through; on the other hand, if he didn't raise any further objection, that could mean that at the end, he and his brother would try to take everything and, if the circumstances were right, kill him and Abe.

"All right, then," Ed said.

Nate felt the hair stand up on the back of his neck. Ed stood up and motioned to his brother that they were leaving. Nate wanted to appear normal and offered his hand to Ed, who looked at it in surprise and then shook hands without any acknowledgment of the normal implications of the act. Abe likewise shook hands with Bump, and the two Hollisters left the little cabin.

"I ain't never been on a train before, Ed," Bump said as soon as they were away from Abe's cabin.

"Just follow Jackson. He's been around. I think he used to be a banker," Ed answered.

Bump grinned. "I guess he musta got tired of handling other people's money."

"He was a paymaster in the war. You're probably right."

Bump got serious. "You mean he never carried a gun?" he asked.

"I doubt it. That's why he wants us. His worthless brother isn't going to be any help."

"Well, I'll follow him, like you say, but I ain't gonna do his laundry!"

"No. And the first time you think he's shining you on, kill

'im! I'm going to try to get more details from Abe Jackson when we come out, and if things go right, we won't need the Jackson brothers."

"Good!"

Ed stopped walking and looked around the street to see if there was anyone within earshot. He was getting an idea that might bestow some advantage on him and his brother. There was another, lesser known Hollister—lesser known because he had spent most of his life in prison. He was likely to be headed back there soon, having beaten two men almost to death in the railroad yards. They had started the fight, but Stanley had finished it, and his previous offenses were going to count against him.

Ed posed a question to his brother. "Is Stan still in jail?"

"He's out on bail. His hearing is next week."

"Let's go talk to him. I'm thinking we might need his help with those Jacksons."

"I know where he's bunking. He's prob'ly there now."

"Let's go."

Nate and Abe sat silently at the table after the Hollisters left. Abe made to pour Nate a drink, but Nate shook his head. "Abe, those two men are rattlesnakes."

"Shoot, I thought I heard something there." Abe made light of Nate's seriousness, grinning to relieve the tension in the room. He grabbed a cup with dice in it and rattled it, his eyes wide.

Nate didn't have his brother's sense of humor. He watched

Abe's face closely as he asked, "What do you do when you hear a rattlesnake?"

Abe's face lost a little of its humor. "You watch where you step and then get out of there."

There was a short silence while each man considered their situation.

"Do you want out of this?" Nate asked. It was a genuine offer. Nate was still new to the business of living outside the law. He was beginning to embrace the fact that his life would forever be more dangerous than it had been when he was living in a small town, working at a small job, and raising a small family. His horizons had definitely expanded since his bungled bank robbery, but so had his risk. He was concerned about both of them surviving.

"Naw, I think it'll work out." Abe rubbed his arms as if he had a chill. "I'd sure like to do right by Penny. We could start over somewhere with that much money."

"All right. Me too," Nate said, although he would be starting over minus the burden of family. He added, "But if you can't get out of the way of a rattlesnake, what's the other thing you do?"

"I've shot a few." Abe shrugged.

"That's right," Nate answered. "These snakes might need shooting too. Keep a gun handy for the next two weeks, brother."

"I'll do that," Abe said, and he made a pistol with his index finger and thumb, aimed it at the floor, and pulled the imaginary trigger. "Poucchh!" he added, imitating a pistol's sound.

Nate stood up and patted his brother on the shoulder. "Here's money for your tickets to Salt Lake, and here's some instructions I've written for you. You can expect the train to stop somewhere before Cheyenne. I'll have to scout for a good spot."

Abe tucked the money and the page of handwriting into his pants pocket. He didn't know what to say to his brother. Things were happening faster than he could keep up with.

Nate sensed that. "We'll do good, Abe. And we'll get rich."

"All right, Nate."

"See you in Cheyenne." Nate slipped out the front door into the night.

Under the bed, Penny had heard everything and was quietly fighting back tears as she formulated a plan of her own.

Chapter Eight

Penny Bradford was an attractive thirty-five-year-old who had supported herself since she was fifteen. She was smart, although lacking in formal education; she was resilient, knew how to take care of herself, and could see farther into her future than most women who worked in her occupation.

Not long before Nate Jackson robbed the bank, she and Abe had one of their more serious conversations.

"Penny," he asked, "when them farm boys dance with you, do they ever try anything?"

Penny was getting dressed to go to work, and she looked at Abe in surprise. *Of course they do.* "Like what?" she asked.

"Ah, you know, grab at you, kinda, or . . . stuff like that."

Penny smiled. "They always grab at me, Abe. That's what I get paid for." She walked to where he was sitting and sat on his lap with one arm around his neck. "Does that bother you?"

"Yeah," he answered. He couldn't look at her, so she put her hand under his chin and tilted his head up. "It doesn't mean anything, Abe. It's just a job."

"It probably don't mean nothin' to them, but it does to me."

"What does it mean to you?"

"Aw, I don't know. I just don't like all them men . . . I wish you didn't do it."

Penny saw that Abe's eyes looked sad. This was probably the most heartfelt thing he had ever said to her. And it was the opening she had been waiting for.

"Did you know that the Union Pacific is hiring? If you got a job there, I could quit the dance hall."

"Aw, Penny, you know I never stick with anything."

"You've stuck with me, Abe Jackson."

Abe grinned. "That was easy." She stood up to resume dressing, but he grabbed her hand and pulled her back. "I mean, I just never wanted to be with another woman after I met you."

She turned to look at him directly. "One of us has to work, Abe. And I don't mean skinning dead cows or running a trapline. One of us has to work steady."

Abe looked at her. She was the best woman he had ever known. "Maybe I'll clean myself up a little and go down and talk to the railroad people."

"You're a good man," she said, and she kissed him on the forehead. She knew she had put as much pressure on him as he could accept. The rest would be up to him.

Penny had supported other men at various times but none for as long as she had Abe. She liked his sense of humor, his recklessness, and his ability to weather any storm, like a fragile glass globe surviving hurricanes on the open sea and bobbing happily on the surface during the calms. She thought there was something more to him than what was apparent on the surface, and she had hopes of a future with him in a more conventional situation—no gambling, no saloons, no dancing, and none of the other things that went with those pursuits. She knew he was at least as smart as she was, but he lacked ambition, save for his loyalty to her. That loyalty, she had always thought, would eventually direct him toward the lifestyle she desired.

But now, after overhearing Nate's plan, she feared that attainment of this lifestyle was in jeopardy if Abe continued to follow his brother. She had no faith that Nate could successfully plan a big robbery, and even if they somehow pulled it off, she had doubts that the money would provide the promised comfort. She had seen too many men strike it rich and, in a short time, have nothing.

As much as she liked Abe, she despised his brother the same. She and Nate had never gotten along. At first it might have been that, as an assistant to the bank manager, he was a respectable member of the Omaha business community and did not want to tarnish his reputation by association with her. He would scarcely acknowledge her when passing on the street, and when she did business with the bank, which was rare, he spoke to her in short, gruff phrases.

What Penny thought now was that Nate wanted control of

his brother, regardless of their different social standing, and he saw Penny as an impediment. She knew most of the details of his botched robbery of the bank that had employed him, and that knowledge told her that he had always been an evil, devious person and had hidden those traits while he worked to advance himself in the banking business. She also knew that when he first came to Omaha, he had been a frequent customer at the dance hall—until one night when he beat one of the dancers unconscious. Then, afraid of being called to account for his actions, he retreated to the respectability of his family and his banking career and never visited the dance hall again. No charges were ever filed, and neither his wife nor his boss was ever made aware of the incident.

Nate had chafed under the autocratic supervision he endured at the bank and the constant nagging of his wife, who couldn't understand why there never seemed to be enough money. When the temptation became too great for him to resist, his respectable lifestyle had ended. So, without the restraint required in his former occupation, he had become as dangerous as any man she had ever met, and that would be a considerable number.

And now the man she was devoted to was preparing to follow this persuasive but evil man, his brother, in a scheme that, in her mind, had disaster written all over it. The best outcome would be that they would succeed, Abe would escape to some location in the far West, and maybe, but only maybe, they would be reunited at some time in the future.

The worst outcome—and the more likely one, she feared—was that Abe would be killed.

Right after Nate slunk away, Abe walked out of their cabin to visit the outhouse. Penny waited for a moment, then crawled out from under the bed, grabbed her shawl, and left, only to return ten minutes later when Abe was brewing a pot of coffee.

"Hey, woman, you off work early?"

Penny didn't want to lie to Abe. She hesitated to answer. Finally he said, "I got some coffee goin'. Want some?"

"Yes," she answered. Then she said, "I saw your brother leaving. What are you two up to?" She tried to keep her voice level and not display the anger and fear she felt. Abe didn't connect the fact that Nate had left a full fifteen minutes before she came home with her statement that she had seen him leave.

"I guess I'm gonna take the train to Cheyenne and give Nate a hand gettin' started out there."

"Is this new start going to be inside the law, or outside?"

Abe grinned, "Well, it might be a little bit of both." He bobbed his head from side to side.

Penny, not amused, was silent.

Abe sensed her distress. "Shoot, it'll be all right, Penny. I'll be back after only a few days," he tried reassuring her. She sat down with her hands in her lap.

"I promise," he added, "it'll be all right. Nate's got it figgered out."

Penny doubted that Nate Jackson had anything figured out. In her opinion he was roping more people into his scheme because he had so little ability of his own. How could two brothers be so different?

Nate Jackson was four years older than Abe and had had the status of only child for those first years. His parents had indulged him and then resented Abe when he was born. As a child, Nate was attractive, precocious, and knew how to please adults. Abe, in contrast, had ears that stuck out, hair that wouldn't comb down, and he stuttered until he reached adolescence. Mrs. Jackson died before Abe started school, and her husband, who was fifteen years her senior, doted on Nate and ignored Abe. Then, when the elder Jackson died, his will left all the family property to the elder son, not an unusual practice in the nineteenth century.

Penny had long ago convinced herself that Nate had advanced in life more because of luck than aptitude. If her Abe had had any of the advantages that Nate had enjoyed, he could have done as well, she was sure. And, unlike his brother, he was a decent person in her estimation. She looked at Abe for a long time.

"Don't go."

"Aw, Penny . . ." Abe didn't know what to say, because he truthfully didn't want to go, but he felt it was his duty. Nate had helped him out many times, and now he could return at least some of that help. But he had a feeling of foreboding that he couldn't shake. His brother had killed a man, something Abe had never done outside of war. If the take was as good as Nate claimed it would be, it seemed almost certain that the cash would be well guarded, and there would be more killing. Even though Abe was not handy with guns, he had no fear he would be killed; he seldom considered his own death. What he feared were the consequences if he were caught. And buried deep within his subconscious was a little, if only a little, moral aversion to taking a human life.

"Don't go," Penny repeated, and she took his hands in hers.

"Nate needs me, Penny. I can't let him down. He's helped me over and over again."

"Then help him get away, but don't go with him. He'll get you killed."

"We'll take care of each other. It'll be all right," he protested. "You'll see."

Penny realized it was fruitless to argue. "I'm going back to the Cattleman's." She carefully walked around him, out of arm's reach. "You'd better figure out where you want your life to go." And she picked up her bag and left.

Abe's shoulders sagged as she walked out. All his doubts were on the surface now. He paced back and forth in the little cabin, but in a few minutes he had come to terms with his situation and sat down to drink his coffee, resigned to the violence that seemed inevitable.

At the Cattleman's dance hall, Penny sought out the manager.

"Jacko, I need to talk to you privately." She glanced around the crowded room.

"Sure, Penny." He took her to his office and closed the door behind them.

"Jacko, would you trade me a little revolver for this?" She produced a Colt's Navy revolver from her bag.

"I suppose so, Penny. What's wrong?"

"I just need to carry something a little handier while I walk back and forth to work." That was a lie. She was planning a course of action to foil Abe's brother, and it featured an easily hidden weapon.

Jacko opened his desk and backed away, bending over, to see far into the top drawer. Then he reached in as he stared at the wall and felt around until he said "Ah," and he withdrew a pocket revolver. "Like this?" he asked.

"Yes, I guess so. It looks awfully small."

"That's what you asked for. But wait, I'll show you something else." He went to a file cabinet, opened a drawer, and withdrew a smaller gun, a two-shot derringer. "This little thing packs a lot bigger punch, but it only holds two shots, and it's not easy to load."

Penny took the derringer that he handed her and looked at it. The hole in the end of the barrel was almost twice that of the little revolver. "This'll do. Trade straight across?"

"Sure, Penny. In fact, you can just have that thing. We took it off a card player we caught cheating. The guys he was playing against beat him up and put him on his horse. I doubt he'll ever come back."

"You might as well take the Navy."

"No, you keep it. You might need it sometime. Are you sure nothing's wrong?" Jacko had always had a soft spot for Penny, the oldest and most dependable of his girls.

"Everything's fine, Jacko. Thanks. I'd better get out there now."

On the floor of the dance hall, Penny leaned over to talk to the piano player. "Henry, I need a coat and hat for a friend of mine who's about your size." Henry was about the same size as Penny. "What did you do with that old ragged cotton duster you used to wear?"

Without missing a note and without taking his eyes off the dancers, Henry answered, "Still got it, I guess."

"If you throw in a hat, any old hat, I'll trade you a good Colt's Navy for it."

Henry glanced quickly at Penny and then again watched the crowd. "Sure, why not? I'll find a good hat for you."

A customer came and took Penny's hand, and they began dancing. At least Penny was dancing; the man was just following her around the dance floor, trying to get both arms around her at the same time. From long practice she had no trouble slipping out of his grasp repeatedly. She usually let the men hold her close, feeling their rough clothes through her flimsy dance costume, but she had no stomach for it tonight.

Jacko thoughtfully watched Penny and the miner dancing and finally went over and cut in, saying, "That's all you get for a dime, my friend. Go get in line again."

The man scowled at Jacko but did as he was told as Jacko and Penny danced away.

"Penny, if you're not going to let the customers dance with you properly, you might as well take the rest of the night off."

"Sorry, Jacko."

"You sure there's nothing wrong?"

"I'm sure."

Jacko beckoned to the man who had gone back to get in line. The man walked over to the couple, and Jacko released Penny, saying, "Why don't you take the rest of my turn, friend? Be good to her, now." The miner gave Jacko a look and then grabbed Penny and began dancing as before, only this time Penny let him pull her close. It was two hours until closing time.

The next evening Henry brought in a jacket and a well-worn hat. Penny gave him her father's Colt's Navy .36 that she had had for nineteen years.

Chapter Nine

This was a part of Omaha that the city fathers would rather not admit to—narrow, muddy streets winding aimlessly through low huts constructed of debris salvaged from the railroad yards. There were few children to play in these muddy streets, and those who did were ragged, dirty, and dour looking. There were no women to be seen, and the men all looked tough and bitter. This neighborhood made Abe and Penny's cabin look palatial. Ed followed Bump through the nameless streets with his right hand in his pocket, on his revolver. Bump stopped at what looked like a packing crate with a door on one end. There were no windows. He knocked on the door.

"Yeah?" came the reply.

"Stan, it's Bump."

"Yeah?" The door opened, and Stan appeared with a gun in

his hand. The top of the doorway came to his nose; he had to stoop to look out at his two brothers. "I thought maybe my bail had been yanked." He grinned wryly.

"Did you beat up someone else?" Bump asked.

"Yeah, some farm boy from downriver." He shook hands with his two brothers.

Ed said, "So they probably *will* revoke your bail."

Stan answered, "Yeah, prob'ly. I was just packin' up to clear out." He turned back into the little hut and returned with a bag that apparently held all his earthly possessions other than the gun in his hand. He stuck the gun in to his belt.

"Where you gonna go, Stan?" Ed asked as the three men walked together in the direction from which Ed and Bump had come.

"I dunno. How've you been, Eddie?"

"Gettin' by. We've got wind of a big job, Stan."

"Need help?"

"That's why we're down here."

"Tell me."

Ed told Stan Hollister what little he knew about the Jacksons' plan: that Bump and Nate Jackson were taking the next train, that he and Abe were following a week later, and that the take would be forty thousand or more.

"And that's all they told you?"

"Yeah, that's it," Ed said. "I can't decide if they're both stupid, or if they're just letting us think that way so they can kill us after we've done our part." Then he added, "Whatever that is."

"Your cards are turned over, and theirs are still hid."

"That's about it," Ed Hollister said. "But we can have one more draw. You."

"How do you want to play it?" Stan asked.

"Let's get off the street. Bump and I have a cabin north of the river landing."

The three brothers walked to the cabin that Ed and Bump shared. There they planned their course of action for the next two weeks. Stan Hollister, certain that by now he was a fugitive, moved in with his brothers and stayed out of sight inside the cabin.

Their plan was not as simple as the Jacksons'. Stan would ride the same train that Bump and Nate rode. He was a stranger to Nate and would remain so. None of the three brothers was deceived by the supposed destination of Salt Lake City. They felt that whatever was going to happen would happen before crossing the continental divide. That seemed to indicate Cheyenne. In any case, Stan would leave the train when Nate did, so that he could keep an eye on him. As soon as he could figure out what Nate was up to, he would kill him, and he and Bump would execute their part of the job. Sometime during the events it would become necessary also to dispose of Abe Jackson. Then the three brothers would divide the forty thousand three ways instead of the five Nate had demanded.

Some days later, Bump Hollister followed a narrow path through low brush until he reached a creek that crossed the path and flowed into the Missouri a mile or so from Omaha. He waded through the swampy creek and found the dead cottonwood on the other side. It looked exactly as Nate Jackson had described it. He looked to his right and picked out the tallest tree on a low ridge that bordered the river. Walking directly toward that tree, as directed, he had to step over and through more low brush that grabbed at his legs. He could tell that he was not the first person to walk this route. Presently he heard his name.

"Hollister?"

"Yeah."

"Bump?" Nate called his first name this time.

"Yeah. Jackson?"

"Walk this way," Nate instructed.

Bump did as he was told, and Nate Jackson stepped from behind a tree in front of him. Bump stopped, and the two men sized each other up briefly. Neither saw anything to like in the other.

"Did you get the tickets?" Nate asked.

Bump pulled a crumpled card from his coat pocket. "Yeah. Here."

Nate looked at the damaged ticket with distaste but took it without words and smoothed it out before putting it into his pocket. Bump looked around in an effort to learn more about this man who had recruited him and his brother. There was nothing to see; Nate's cold camp was hidden in a thicket one hundred yards away.

"Is the train on time?" Nate asked.

"Yeah. I'm gonna go get my bag and wait at the station. You comin'?"

"No. I've got some things to do, but I'll be there when the

train comes in." What Nate didn't want to tell Bump, even though it must have been fairly obvious, was that he couldn't afford to be seen in Omaha. He would remain hidden in the river bottom and would not board the train until the last moment.

"Suit yourself. I'm headin' out," Bump said.

Nate made no reply, and Bump turned to retrace his steps.

An hour later Nate was walking alleys and back streets as he made his way to the Omaha train station, valise in hand. The sun was well up, and this was the first time he had walked through Omaha in daylight since the robbery. He walked with his bald head uncovered; people who knew him, knew him with a full head of hair. He also carried his head erect to display his beard. There was nothing in his posture or his gait that suggested a man afraid to be seen, and that was what he wanted. He was just another traveler taking the train west.

The train was at the depot. This was the start of the line, as there was no way to get a train across the Missouri River between Council Bluffs and Omaha. On the east side of the river the train from Chicago was turned around and making its way back east. The omnibus from the ferry landing had already dropped all the passengers at the station. A few of these were staying in Omaha; most were continuing west. As it was a nice day, most passengers and people meeting arriving travelers were on the platform. That being the case, Nate decided to wait inside the depot and entered a side door. He watched the people on the platform from a window. Bump was nowhere in sight.

The departing passengers were starting to board. Nate, still wondering where Bump might be, strode quickly across the platform and climbed into a car. He found a seat on the platform side, where he could observe.

Bump had been given more money for the tickets than their cost. He hadn't bothered to inform Nate Jackson of that fact when they met in the river bottom, and when he left Nate, he had gone directly to a little house he knew of where there was always a card game in progress. It took him only minutes to lose his little windfall, so he was in a foul mood when he left to catch the train.

As Bump hurried through the depot, he collided with a man standing on the platform next to the door. The man was sent sprawling on the platform. Bump didn't stop to apologize.

"Hey," the man said as he picked himself up, "watch where you're going, you big ox!"

Bump stopped, turned, and went back to the man. The man immediately began backing up but in vain. Bump smashed his fist into the man's face, breaking his nose. The unfortunate man went down, his face covered in blood, but Bump was not satisfied. He leaned over the man, lifting him by his collar, and then slammed him back onto the platform. As a final gesture, Bump kicked him hard in the ribs.

There were only a few people left on the platform by that time, but they saw what had happened and reacted in horror. Bump glared at each of them in turn as if to say, *So what!* and they retreated. The whistle on the engine blew, and Bump ran and jumped onto a step as the train started moving.

Nate had witnessed the incident. He wished the man had shot Bump. He was beginning to believe that Bump Hollister was going to be more of a liability than an asset. At least he hadn't paired Bump with his brother, Abe. Abe was too good-natured and easygoing; he would never have been able to protect himself from Bump. Nate, however, thought he knew exactly what he was up against, what kind of evil giant Bump Hollister was turning out to be, and he was prepared to not just defend himself but to take action before he was even threatened, if he thought that to be best.

There was another interested witness to Bump's brutality. Stan Hollister had boarded the train right after it pulled into the station. When he saw Bump beat the unfortunate traveler, he grinned to himself. His little brother, Bump, was a beast.

Chapter Ten

Mary Ann Bringham stood next to her luggage on the platform. It had been a lovely spring day in New York City, and now the sun was only a few diameters above the horizon. Her grandparents were there to see her off, her grandmother asking questions, concerned for her welfare. "Do you have your ticket? . . . Will you wire us from Chicago? . . . "Is your jewelry case inside your suitcase?"

Her grandfather walked along the platform inspecting the locomotive. He had been an engineer for the railroad until he retired after the war at the age of seventy-one. The advances in steam engine technology had been considerable since then.

Mary Ann looked at her grandmother with great tenderness. She was small and frail, a shawl wrapped around her round shoulders, and her thin white hair exposed to the eve-

ning, which was becoming cool. Mary Ann lifted the shawl a
little on the back of her grandmother's head. A porter Mary
Ann had signaled came to her and handed her two luggage
checks. Then he hefted her two large suitcases without any
strain and carried them toward the baggage car.

"If there's time, I'll wire you. I only have an hour between
trains there." She pulled two hatboxes closer, now that her
suitcases were gone. "Now, don't worry if you don't hear
from me Wednesday. I should have plenty of time to get off a
telegram in Omaha."

Her grandfather rejoined them. "I can't see why they
changed that slide valve the way they did. I'll be watching as
they pull out to see just how it works." He was purposely dis-
tracting himself from the reality of his granddaughter's leaving. He didn't want to think that he would probably never
see her again.

"Pop, you ought to say something to your granddaughter,"
her grandmother said as she looked up at her husband. He
glanced back at the drivers on the locomotive and then looked
at Mary Ann.

"You tell my son-in-law that we want you back here real
soon," he said, putting his hands on her shoulders and facing
her squarely. "You're too pretty a young lady for the West.
We want you back here," he repeated. He tried to sound stern,
but his voice was unsteady.

The conductor cried, "All aboard!"

The old man wrapped his precious granddaughter in his
arms briefly and then released her. She in turn hugged her
grandmother and then looked around to the door of her car.

The conductor beckoned her, and she left her grandparents to board the impatient train. Most of the other passengers were already on board, but she had waited until the last moment. As she stepped up into the car, the conductor waved at a brakeman and then followed Mary Ann into the car.

The brakemen up and down the line signaled the engineer, the whistle on the locomotive blew, and the drivers that her grandfather had been so interested in began to turn, yanking the slack out of the couplings with a series of bangs. He was oblivious to the mechanism he had expressed interest in only moments ago. He was standing with his arm around his wife, watching his granddaughter's face at the window of her car as the train slowly left the station.

Mary Ann watched from her seat in the Pullman car, her face pressed against the glass, looking back, as the two figures grew smaller. Only then did her emotions get the best of her, and she put a gloved hand to her face. She would not let herself think that after six years of life with her grandparents, she might never see them again.

She stayed at the window and watched as the waterfront of New York passed by. Masts of the tall ships at anchor looked like a dead forest, the ratlines and rigging like huge spider trails draped from the tops of the trees down to some strange kind of geometric shrubbery surrounding them.

Her life in Eastern society was at an end, and that fact did not in the least bring her sorrow. She would miss her grandparents, who had taken care of her for almost six years as she completed school and college, but she knew that from now on she had to be her own person, whether in the East with them or in the West with her father, whom she hadn't seen in all that time. She would miss her friends also. There were girlfriends with whom she had studied and socialized; there were boys who had courted her, all unsuccessfully. There were her professors, some with whom she had been close, getting advice and guidance from them—the kind of advice that she couldn't get from her grandparents or her young friends. And she also wrote to her father, who always had the last word as far as she was concerned.

The train rattled over a switch as it reached the limits of the yard, and she nearly hit her head on the window, so closely was she watching the passing scenes. She pulled back from the window a little, and the train rattled over another switch. The train was picking up speed, and she became dizzy trying to focus on objects it was passing. She had to look away for a moment, but then, as the track seemed to smooth out, she again directed her attention to the window and found the speed exhilarating.

So there would be new friends, new things to learn, very likely a different social structure, perhaps some romance, certainly adventure and excitement. When she thought about all those things, her pulse quickened. She was more than ready for a change. She had to tell herself to let the future stay in the future for now. She would not want to miss the details of this train trip while she engaged in pointless daydreaming. As she watched the last of New York slip by her window, she removed her diary from her purse, wrote a few lines, and then put it away.

The track was smooth through the countryside west of

New York, and she again pressed her face to the window and settled down to watch the ever-changing view. The train made slow progress on this section, and she had time to observe in detail the farms and settlements near the track. Although the train was traveling slowly, it seemed to her to be with amazing speed—over twenty miles an hour! In a few days she would be even more amazed when the track was straighter and more level as it crossed the plains and greater speeds were realized.

There came a sound of someone clearing his throat, and she looked around to see the conductor waiting patiently to gain her attention. She looked up at him.

"Could I see your ticket, please, ma'am?" he asked.

She could smell the camphor in his uniform and also the faint odor of starch in his shirt. His eyes looked kind, and Mary Ann decided he was a patient person.

"Yes, of course." She withdrew the ticket from her bag and handed it to him, watching his face.

What an interesting job he had, she thought. He would soon have spoken to everyone in this car and would no doubt have opinions about most of them; certainly *she* would, if she were checking tickets. He punched one hole in her ticket and handed it back to her. She wondered how long he would be on this train. She would be on it for several days, and she hoped he would be also; he seemed to be the kind of person one could rely on in a time of need. Not that she expected any trouble, but there was a mountain of unknown ahead of her. He touched his hat and moved to the next person to repeat the process.

The Pacific Express on which Mary Ann rode would travel

all night to arrive in Rochester in the morning. From there it would cross Niagara Falls and enter Canada, traveling near the north shore of Lake Erie to Windsor. Then the entire train would board a ferry to be taken across the Detroit River and once again be in the United States, arriving in Chicago two and a half days from its departure from New York. There were three routes to Chicago, all the same price, and Mary Ann had chosen this one, it being the most scenic.

Chapter Eleven

Nate Jackson was standing at the car door when the train stopped in Cheyenne. He had no baggage, only a small grip containing a change of clothes, a pistol, and a break-down shotgun wrapped in a piece of blanket. Around his waist was a money belt containing the remnants of his inept bank robbery and his savings from the honest work he would never do again. He immediately spotted a man with a badge standing on the platform two cars down. He stepped onto the platform and walked directly into the station, through the building, and onto Main Street, and then, seeing the hotel, walked in that direction.

Nate had managed to slip Bump a note telling him to get off the train at Cheyenne and check into the hotel, but nothing more. Minutes after he stepped off the train, Bump Hollister stepped off as instructed. They had not spoken to each other on the train, and they would register at the hotel separately.

From his seat Stan Hollister watched Nate cross the platform quickly. When he saw Bump also get off, he felt sure that this was their destination, but he waited until the whistle blew before jumping up from his seat and quickly stepping off the train. He crossed the platform to try to keep Nate in sight. He needed a place to spend the night. The three brothers had scraped all their money together for his rail ticket, and he had not enough left for a room. No matter. He had food and water in his bag, and when the sun got low in the west, he would find a place somewhere in a shed on the outskirts. He had one task before he left town. He went to the telegraph office and sent a telegram to his brother, Ed, in Omaha.

GOT OFF CHEYENNE. DANCE IS HERE.

Telegrams were expensive, so it was not unusual for senders to leave out as many words as possible, confusing the meaning for anyone but the recipient. The telegrapher, accustomed to the abbreviated language after years of telegraphy, was nonetheless confused by this message.

"That's it?" he asked.

"That's it," Stan affirmed. He paid the man and left quickly, walking east along the tracks.

Checking into the hotel, Nate signed the name *Ned Johnson* on the register. His unneeded eyeglasses worked well at close range, making his signature look bigger than it was.

"Do you have baggage at the station, Mr. Johnson?" the clerk asked.

"No." Nate looked at his grip, then added, "I'll only be staying until next week."

He had started to say, *"next week's train,"* then thought better of it. He would actually be out of Cheyenne before the train was due to arrive in order to stop it somewhere on the eastern side of Cheyenne. Letting the clerk believe he would still be in Cheyenne when the train arrived shouldn't have made any difference, but the fewer details he supplied, true or not, the less he would have to remember as he dealt with people in town. Although not a career criminal until just recently, he nevertheless was clever, sly, and quick to learn how to lie convincingly.

"Very well, sir." The clerk handed him a key. "Your room is on the ground floor, down the hall on the right."

Nate picked up the key without thanking the clerk and walked down the hallway to his room.

Once inside the room, he locked the door, checked that the window was latched, pulled the shade, and removed his coat and shirt. He took some money from his money belt for meals and to purchase some of the materials he would need. He looked at his face in the mirror and rubbed his shaved head. He decided he had better shave again soon and removed his shaving supplies from his grip. After he was satisfied with his appearance, he donned his shirt and coat and left his room to walk through town.

A breeze blowing along Main Street in Cheyenne raised little dust devils, and if someone galloped a horse down the street, a small dust cloud was generated and then absorbed by the buildings, the animals, and the pedestrians. This was the first western town Nate had visited, and it seemed not that different, although smaller, than his hometown of Omaha, both being relatively new settlements. Omaha was a crossroads of the Missouri River and the railroad; Cheyenne was a crossroads of the railroad and a wagon trail.

Nate's first stop was the livery stable, where he hired a wagon and a team of two mules. The stable hand asked several times what he needed the rig for, but Nate evaded the question. The stable hand harnessed the mules and then hitched them to the wagon while Nate watched, only occasionally lending a hand when it was obvious what was needed. Holding the reins firmly in his hand, the stable hand addressed Nate.

"I reckon I'd better get a deposit on this here rig, since yore a stranger 'bouts."

"Very well. Will twenty dollars be sufficient?"

"That'd be about right, I reckon. I'll have to get my wife to make out a receipt."

"That won't be necessary." Nate's plans did not include returning the rig, and he hadn't even thought about getting a receipt for his deposit. Then he realized he should not conduct his business any differently than if he were an ordinary citizen and amended his statement. "Maybe I should get a receipt. I'll just wait here if you'll have your wife take care of it."

The stable hand thought the man's sudden change peculiar, but he just said, "Shore. I'll be back in a jiffy." And he walked away to take care of the receipt.

When Nate had the receipt, he drove the rig around onto Main Street and stopped in front of a hardware store. He wanted some specific tools, but he had to buy other tools to make it appear as if he had legitimate intentions. He presented his list to Ralph Iverson, the proprietor, who studied it for a moment. Iverson also wanted to know what Nate was going to do.

"Prospecting?" he asked.

Nate just shrugged silently.

"Ya know, there isn't any gold 'round here."

Nate didn't smile at the unintended irony. "We'll see."

Ralph wanted to ask more, but he had dealt with prospectors before, and the only time they talked, in his experience, was when they didn't know anything. "You'll have to go to the gunsmith for the black powder."

"Very well."

"And I don't have blankets. The general store will have 'em."

"All right. Fix me up with what you do have."

"Yes, sir." And he began walking around his store, picking up pieces of merchandise and bringing them back to the counter: a cooking pot, a large pry bar, a sledgehammer, a lantern and coal oil, an axe, a coil of rope, a tarpaulin, a shovel, a pickax, a wedge for wood splitting. "I only have these big fry pans," he said, pointing to a large frying pan hanging on a nail. "The general store has several sizes."

"All right."

Ralph didn't know if that meant, *"All right, I'll take that one,"* or, *"All right, I'll buy one at the general store,"* so he made a point of walking away from the frying pan he had indicated to find the next item. At about that time the front door opened, and Marshal Bringham came in.

Nate recognized the marshal as the man with the badge he had seen on the station platform. He instinctively turned away and then realized it made no difference, so he turned back toward Bringham and met his gaze, nodding.

Brink nodded and then addressed Ralph. "Ralph, how's the hardware business today?"

Nate was suspicious of this question. Did the marshal see the pile of tools on the counter, and was he trying to find out what Nate was going to do with them?

"Well, Brink, it's been up and down. The Army doesn't spend as much here as it used to. A lot of their supplies come direct to them by train now."

Brink smiled. "That's progress, Ralph. You gotta take the good with the bad, right?"

"Oh, sure. The good part is that I get supplies in three to four weeks now. I used to have to order six months ahead."

"Well, there you go." Brink smiled. He casually walked past the counter that held Nate's supplies. Nate noticed and frowned. "Speaking of that, did those nuts and bolts I ordered come in?"

"The UP sent me a note that I had some freight at the station. In the morning I'll send Bobby down with a cart to bring everything up here. If it's not with that batch . . . next week, maybe, huh?"

"Yeah, it's not terribly important. I need to replace the bolts that hold the bars in the jail to the floor, you know." Brink winked at Nate as if he knew him personally and then added, "We wouldn't want any bad guys to escape, would we?"

Nate was not amused and couldn't keep his face from showing distaste.

This was not lost on Brink. He was standing close to Nate and met his gaze, eye to eye, trying to read the man's character, purpose, or personality. He came to no conclusion, but something about the man's face seemed familiar.

He tried to draw him into a conversation. "Looks like you got a big job ahead of you somewhere, mister." He nodded toward the tools. "If you need some help, I can steer you to some pretty good hands."

Nate had to force himself to smile thinly. "I'll keep that in mind, Marshal." He didn't elaborate.

Brink nodded as if he understood, but he understood nothing. The man had selected an odd mix of tools. He waved at Ralph and left the store.　.

Nate released the breath he'd been holding. He needed to think about how to shed the marshal and not call more attention to himself.

Back at the hotel Nate casually looked over the register and saw the signature, *B. Hollis.* He knew that was Bump. The clerk had written in the room number, 10, which was just across from Nate's room. Nate walked down the first-floor hallway, looked back over his shoulder, saw no one, and tapped on the door to room number ten. In a moment the door was opened by Bump, and Nate quickly stepped in.

"'Bout time you showed up," Bump growled, shutting the

door. His room was tiny, and the window looked out on an alley.

"I've got a wagon and most of the supplies." Nate was thinking fast. Bump was big, over six feet tall, strong, and obviously accustomed to doing whatever he felt like doing. The preparations that Nate had estimated would take several days were mostly done. It had seemed like a good idea to allow plenty of time out here in the unknown West to gather the equipment necessary to rob a train—no simple task—but if he could have moved the date forward, he would have. They could stay in town six days and then meet the train at the place of his choosing east of town. But there was trouble all over Bump's face. He was already impatient and restless. Nate made a quick decision; they would camp on the prairie for a few days. "We'll check out in the morning and head out with the wagon."

"You said we'd be here five days!" Bump nearly shouted. "I ain't even got comfortable, and there's a dance hall down the street that's sayin', 'Bump, we got just what you need.'" Bump grinned in anticipation.

"I changed the plan," Nate said, irritated.

"Well, what the heck *is* the plan?" Bump shouted.

"The plan, my friend, is for you to stay in this hotel room until I need you," Nate said quietly and deliberately. "You can go to the café, and that's all. Don't talk to anyone. Don't go anywhere else. Don't attract attention." Nate knew that Bump would not follow the orders as soon as he uttered them. What to do?

"Nope. I'm goin' to that there dance hall. You stay here and change your plan all you want."

Chapter Twelve

Jimmy watched from the passenger car as his horses were led to the loading chute of a livestock car. It was just past four in the morning, and the gaslights at the station platform in Fort Wayne, fighting the dark blue of the sky to the east, barely allowed him to see what was happening. But he could tell that the men doing the work were not being rough with the horses and were talking to them, coaxing them, and gently pushing them from outside the rails of the chute, which satisfied Jimmy.

The horses, a good saddle, a Colt conversion pistol, and a new pair of boots were all he owned in the world now—plus a railroad ticket to Cheyenne, where he hoped he had a job waiting.

He had been a bit liberal with the truth when writing to the marshal. His claim that he had four years' experience as a peace officer was based on the fact that he had spent those years as a self-appointed peace officer in Marion, and no one in town seemed to mind. Marion had no real need for law enforcement other than to run errands for the tax department, which Jimmy frequently did, but a few of the townspeople felt that it was not a bad thing to have a young man with a badge and a revolver at his side walk through the tiny town once in a while.

His old gelding had walked up the chute to the livestock car, and the others were now following him.

Jimmy had had plenty of time to consider his future as he led the string of horses from Marion to Fort Wayne. The reply from Marshal Bringham had, in his mind, been encouraging. He was certain that he would be able to secure a position with the marshal and begin his career in law enforcement. If not, he would become a bounty hunter. He had read of their exploits many times in the periodicals that were sent down from Chicago. And he would also breed the finest horses the West had ever seen.

Men would come hundreds of miles to purchase his horses. He wouldn't sell to just anyone, though. He had decided that he would never sell a horse to an outlaw; that would give him an unfair advantage over his pursuers, of which he might be one. He would sell only to the Army, peace officers, and wealthy ranchers, who would spread the word of the quality of his animals and ultimately make him famous as a breeder.

His mind turned to his farewell at the farm. His two brothers had helped him gather the horses he desired, and they both wished him well at the gate. In the weeks since he had announced his departure, it seemed that the three of them had become closer.

"You still have five good mares here, Jimmy," Richard, the oldest, had said. "Are you going to come back for them?"

"No. They belong to the farm. If I were you, I'd keep them and wait for that stallion to get a little older. He might turn out to be the best one to breed."

"We'll save them for you as long as we can, but I don't think we'll be doing any horse breeding while you're gone," Richard said.

"Are you ever coming back, Jimmy?" Ronald had asked. It had suddenly struck both brothers that Jimmy was not only a buffer between them and their father, he was also the odd ingredient that made the family soup more palatable. He was the one who broke the silence at the dinner table, the one who never failed to comment on a beautiful sunrise, the one who would put a coat of paint on something, not just for protection but to make it look better.

"Jimmy, when you get to Cheyenne, get some gold and send it back to us," Richard said.

Before Jimmy could reply, Ronald said, "No, send us a couple of those California women." They all smiled, a rare occasion. Neither of Jimmy's brothers had a grasp of the geography of the West. They assumed that Cheyenne and San Francisco were as close to each other as Washington, D.C., and Baltimore.

"Probably the best I'll be able to do is send you a handful

of dirt," Jimmy said. "Then you can scatter it in the cornfield and tell everyone that you've plowed Wyoming earth."

Their smiles broadened. Jimmy's father had walked up then. "James, these boys have work to do."

"These boys," Richard and Ronald, were in their thirties, but all three would always be boys to Jonas Whipwell. Richard and Ronald took the cue, and each gave Jimmy a warm handshake and then left to do his chores.

"Well," Jonas had said, "I, uh . . ." He watched his two older sons walk away.

Jimmy extended his hand. "Father," he said.

His father had ignored his outstretched hand. There was something on his mind, and when Jimmy realized that fact, he dropped his arm and waited.

"I think you should have this, James."

It was a picture of Jimmy's mother at the front door of their home, taken the year she died. This was the family's only picture of her; Jonas was not one to waste money on such frivolous things as photographers. Jimmy took the picture and looked at it carefully. She was more beautiful than he remembered. His father patted him on the back without a word and turned to join his other two sons. There was always work to be done.

Jimmy was brought back to reality by a release of steam from the engine. His horses were startled, but they were well controlled by the men and the loading chute and quickly settled down again as the stallions entered the stock car. The men removed the bridge to the chute and closed the door to

the car. A brakeman came up and talked briefly to the loading crew, then released the brake on the car. He signaled the
engine with his lantern and climbed onto the ladder. Up the
line the signal was repeated by another brakeman, and soon
the train began to move. The view from the window grew
darker and then went black, and Jimmy settled into his seat
to sleep until the train arrived in Chicago.

When the train stopped in Fort Wayne, Mary Ann awoke in
her berth. For a moment she couldn't remember where she
was. She had awakened several times in the night, but the mo-
tion of the train at those times had immediately made her
aware of where she was. This time there was silence, and it
caused her some confusion for an instant. Then she remembered and rolled over to pull the curtains aside on the tiny
window in her compartment.

She saw a small depot and a freight shed sharing the platform. A young man led a string of nine horses up onto the
platform and handed the lead's halter to a railroad worker.
They conversed for a moment, and the young man walked to
a passenger car, not a Pullman. Mary Ann felt sympathy for
him; he would have to try to sleep on a padded bench. She
hoped he was only going as far as Chicago, to spare him
days of discomfort in the coach, but the way he was dressed
seemed to hint at a destination far to the west. He wore riding boots, a wide-brimmed hat, and had a revolver strapped
around his waist. In fact, he looked a lot like the drawings
she had seen in magazines of cowboys in Texas.

When Mary Ann heard the whistle, she braced her feet

against the end of her compartment, having several times experienced the lurch of the car as the train began moving. She could hear the bangs of the couplings, and then her body was driven back against the partition as her car abruptly started. She heard the person in the compartment ahead of her hit the partition and cry out softly. Then the few lights of Fort Wayne were gone, and the clicking of the track bespoke the acceleration of the Pacific Express.

Chapter Thirteen

Brink could see the stranger's wagon parked at the side of the hotel. He had not seen the man since the hardware store encounter, and he wanted another look at his face so he could determine why that face seemed so familiar. He crossed the street and entered the hotel lobby to question the clerk about the man.

"Leo, have you seen the man who's driving that wagon?" he asked the clerk.

"No, Marshal, not today. The wagon hasn't moved for over a day. He might be down in his room; do you want to try the door? He's in number eight."

"No, I guess not. Thanks, Leo. I need to be looking in at the bars. Likely he'll be hanging out in one of them."

"Very well, Marshal. Good evening, then."

Nate had been standing in the hall, which was not visible

from the front desk, and heard the short conversation. One of his skills was observing without being observed, developed in the political atmosphere of the bank he had worked for those many years. Why was the marshal interested in him? What had gone wrong? He was tempted to walk quietly through town to find Bump and see if he was staying out of trouble. Now it seemed more prudent to stay in his room. He slipped up the stairs so he could get a view of the street from the upstairs hallway. The clerk didn't notice.

Brink looked in the windows of the café as he walked the boardwalk. He noted with satisfaction that April was still working there. He hadn't talked to her since the Monday morning that he had released her from house arrest and then walked her to the café, where he had introduced her to the owner. He felt good that his effort on her behalf seemed to be producing good results. He continued on down the board-walk to the Main Street Saloon.

Inside the saloon he had a brief conversation with Sam, and then, because things were quiet, he excused himself and continued down the boardwalk to the Frontier Dance Hall. He got there just in time.

As Brink walked in, a bottle crashed into the wall next to the door. He moved quickly sideways as he sized up the room, his hand on his gun in its holster. The next thing coming his way was a chair, which landed to one side, and this time he saw the man who'd thrown it, a young cowboy who was trying in vain to slow the advance of a hulk of a man.

The big man reached for the cowboy just as Slim, the

bartender, smashed his club against the back of the hulk's head. The man stared straight ahead, took a deep breath, and then turned around, a wicked grin coming over his face. The blow he had just received seemed to have produced more annoyance than injury. He grabbed Slim by the throat as Brink stepped up and put the barrel of his gun against the man's ear.

"Whoa, big fella. Better turn him loose now," Brink advised.

Bump dropped Slim and faced the marshal, still grinning. "Sure, Marshal. We's just havin' fun."

"Well, now, how about having a seat while I figure out who's having the most fun here?"

Bump, still grinning, sat heavily in a chair, which creaked in protest.

Brink looked at Slim, who was just picking himself up off the floor. "What's the deal, Slim?"

Slim stood up slowly, rubbing his throat and trying to swallow so that he could speak. He waved Brink to wait while he gathered himself. He pointed at the cowboy who had been defending himself against Bump. Hoarsely, he spoke. "I'm thinkin' that that there cowboy was cheatin' at cards. I couldn't tell from behind the bar, and I was just coming around to check on him when he got into it with the big man."

"Now, that just ain't true, Marshal," the cowboy protested. "It was that big fella was doin' the cheatin'."

Brink turned to Bump, who was still sitting in the chair. "How about it, buddy?"

Bump smiled up at Brink and said, "Well, Marshal, I reckon if I was cheatin', I'd be cheatin' to win."

"That's right, Marshal." One of the other card players spoke up. "The only one who's been winning is that fella there." He pointed at the cowboy. "Bump ain't won a hand since I set down."

Brink looked at the accused cowboy. "Your name is Rex, isn't it?"

"Yeah," he replied.

"All right, Rex. I've been hearing about you. Pick up your winnings, and hit the road. This card game's over." Brink wasn't smiling, and such was his reputation in town that no one argued. Each scraped his own chips off the table, and some went to the bar, while some walked out into the night.

Bump was still sitting in the chair, his arms folded across his chest. "What about me, Marshal?"

"You're Bump, right?"

"Yes, sir, since I was four years old."

Brink could easily imagine how he had gotten such a name. "Where're you from, Bump?"

"East."

"You got a job here?"

"Lookin', Marshal." Bump grinned widely, "You need a deputy?"

In other circumstances Brink might have been tempted. The man's bulk and ability to absorb punishment could be a real asset. And Brink was always drawn to men with a sense of humor. But something told Brink that this man was too much of a troublemaker to be of value as a peace officer.

"I'm going to put you in jail for the night, Bump," the marshal said, not unkindly. It was partly for Bump's safety, partly to calm the atmosphere in the bar. Then he added in the same friendly tone, "If I hadn't walked in when I did, you might have killed Slim, and he's a friend of mine."

Bump's face clouded over. For a minute it looked as if he might make a move against the marshal, and Brink tensed up to be ready.

Instead, Bump commented in a steady, serious voice. "That don't seem right, Marshal. If I hadn't done something, that cowboy, Rex, would've cleaned us all out."

Several men, including the bartender, nodded assent.

"The card game's over, Bump," the marshal said. "I'm going to give you a room for the night so that no one starts a rougher game."

Bump shrugged, resigned to his fate. "All right, you're the marshal," he said. Then he grinned and asked, "I've lost my eatin' money. How's your food?"

"I'll keep you fed, Bump. Supper tonight, breakfast in the morning, then we'll go see the judge. Are you carrying a gun?"

"Left it in my hotel room. What's the judge gonna do?"

"I'll put in a good word for you. I don't think the city wants to feed you for very long." The marshal and Bump both smiled. "Is your room locked?"

"Yeah, Marshal."

"Let's go, then."

Bump stood up, and he and the marshal walked out together. On the boardwalk they met Bob, Brink's deputy. One of the patrons at the saloon had run to get him when the trouble first started.

"Got a customer for you, Bob. We'll put him up for the night."

As the three men walked past the café, Brink looked in and called to April that he needed an evening meal at the jail. It was late, but he knew she would find something for his prisoner.

Nate was still at the window observing the street. He had heard the ruckus in the dance hall and watched as the marshal and then his deputy went in to deal with it. He knew that Bump was in there and hoped that he was not involved. When he saw the two peace officers escorting Bump to the jail, he cursed under his breath. Now what? If Bump were in for more than a few days, he would be worthless to Nate. Even worse, he might inadvertently say something to tip the marshal to their plans. The sooner he was out of jail, the better. The other option was to kill him, but then Nate would have to handle his end of the train robbery alone. Nate returned to his room to think this over.

After Bump was locked away, the marshal told Bob to go home and come back after midnight to spend the night with the prisoner. In the meantime, Brink could walk the town and keep an eye on the jail.

Nate walked quietly across the hall to Bump's room. He had no difficulty forcing the door open. Using the pry bar he had just bought, he spread the flimsy door frame enough to let the door swing in. He quickly entered and eased the door shut behind himself.

Bump had few belongings. Nate pulled the shade and then lit a lamp. His plan was to help Bump break out of jail and get him out of town. Bump could hide out somewhere near the spot of the intended train robbery. He would have to reveal to Bump more of the plan, but that shouldn't make much difference at this late date.

Nate took only Bump's gun and a leather bag containing balls, powder, and caps. He reasoned that if he cleaned the room out, the marshal would realize that someone in town—indeed, someone in the hotel—had helped Bump escape. That was supposing, of course, that Bump could successfully break out.

Nate peeked into the hotel lobby and found it empty. He walked out into the night with Bump's revolver under his coat. Taking side streets and alleys, he found the back of the jail. He waited in the shadows until he heard the marshal exit from the front.

The window in the cell was high and narrow, and there was nothing to stand on. Nate reached for the sill and, with difficulty, pulled himself up so that he could see into the cell.

"Bump!" he said in a low voice. "Bump!" he repeated.

"Yeah?" came the answer from within the cell.

"Get over to the window."

"Nate?"

Nate's strength had run out, and he had to let himself down to the ground. Bump's face appeared at the window.

"Is that you, Nate?"

"What did you do?"

Bump chuckled. "I had to give a guy a lesson in playing poker."

Nate cursed under his breath. It would do no good to point out to Bump that this was the very reason he should not have gone to the dance hall.

"You've got to get out of there."

"Yeah, I think I'll be out in a day or two."

If Nate thought about it, that probably would not spoil his plan. It was now Wednesday evening. He wouldn't need Bump until Friday, when they would ride out to the selected holdup spot and begin working on the track. But Nate was afraid to leave Bump alone in the jail. Bump liked to talk, and the marshal was very observant. And Nate was not patient; he couldn't let matters take their own course. He was becoming ever more anxious about his scheme, and Bump was frustrating him.

"I want you out of there tonight."

That was all right with Bump. "That'd tickle me."

Nate remembered the marshal's remark in the hardware store that the bolts holding the bars to the floor were in need of replacing. He still had the pry bar that he had used to open Bump's room.

"Here, take this stuff." Nate pushed Bump's pistol, ammunition, and the pry bar up through the window's bars.

"Try the pry bar on the floor plate where the cell bars are fastened to the floor. They'll pop out, I'm sure. When you get out, head east down the rail line. I'll bring some food, water, and blankets to you. The marshal is gone now, so hurry."

Bump snorted in amusement. The cell was like a huge upside-down basket woven from iron straps and riveted together. The roof of the cell was lower than the ceiling of the room. He had already seen how the bars were fastened, and, if it hadn't been for the free meals, he would have ripped them off the floor before now. He did exactly that while Nate slunk back through the alleys and side streets to the hotel, where he took up his vantage point to watch the street. He wanted to make sure that Bump managed to escape without incident.

The town of Cheyenne had quieted down since the brawl in the dance hall. The marshal checked the doors of the closed businesses as he walked along the boardwalk. The café was closed now, but through the window he could see April working in the kitchen. She had carved out a place for herself and was doing well. Brink felt a measure of satisfaction at that.

There were still two bars open, but there was no activity in either of them. Brink went into the Frontier Dance Hall and sat down at the bar. "Things look pretty quiet, now, Slim," he commented.

"Yeah," Slim replied as he washed glasses. "I don't know which causes the most trouble, card playing or dance girls."

"Drinking," was the marshal's terse reply.

Slim smiled. "I guess I'll have to put up with that. I sure wouldn't want to go back to gandy dancing."

"I heard you were a section foreman."

"It's all the same—hot sun, cold winds, hard rain. Big,

tough guys who don't like to take orders. This is better." The marshal nodded, and Slim added, "I might look around and get me a bigger stick, though, speaking of big, tough guys."

"You hit Bump pretty hard, and he shook it off," the marshal said.

"You got him locked up now?"

"Yeah."

And that reminded Brink that he needed to return to the jail. It was nearing midnight.

"I'm headed back to the jail, Slim. Are you closing soon?"

"Soon as I finish cleaning up," Slim replied.

Brink slapped the bar and walked back out into the night. Down the street he saw Bob, his deputy, coming back to work, to sit with the prisoner all night.

Bump looked around the office after he got out of the cell. Maybe, he thought, there was something here he could use. The marshal had left a lamp burning low; Bump turned it up and opened each drawer in the marshal's desk. He found some tobacco, which he put in his pocket, but nothing else of interest. He shuffled the papers on the marshal's desk, but since he could read only poorly, he lost interest in them. Then he looked up at the wall above and saw the WANTED poster for Nate Jackson.

"How about that?" he said out loud to himself.

He looked around on the marshal's desk, found a pencil, and drew a mustache and beard on Nate's likeness. He stepped back to admire his work, finding great amusement in it. Then, using the pencil as a spear, he jammed it into

Nate's forehead and imbedded the point in the soft wood of the wall. That made him laugh out loud.

"Take that, Jackson!"

Bump walked to the gun rack. There was one Henry repeating rifle, a shotgun, and several muzzle loaders. They were secured in the cabinet by a steel bar through the trigger guards. The bar was padlocked into place. Bump was deciding on the best way to smash the rack and remove the repeater when he heard steps on the boardwalk outside.

At the hallway window of the hotel Nate was raging. The fool Hollister had not managed to clear the jail, and now a man, probably a deputy, was unlocking the front door and preparing to enter. The jailbreak was going to fail. He had a gun in his room, but there was no time to get it. In any case, he knew that to get directly involved with Bump's escape would put him at risk. He realized that the best thing that could happen now would be for the deputy or the marshal to kill Bump as he tried to make good his escape.

As Bob fumbled to find the right key for the front door, he saw the marshal walking toward him.

"Anything going on, Brink?"

"No. Just the prisoner in there."

"Might as well go on home. I'll see you in the morning."

"Sure. I just wanted to take one more look at our tenant." The marshal continued walking toward the jail.

Bob found the key and inserted it in the lock. When he released the latch, the door burst open, and he was knocked down into the street. Bump stepped out and was about to give Bob a hard kick to the head.

"Hold it!" Brink shouted.

"Aw, Marshal," Bump said, grinning, "you're always spoiling my fun." Bump turned to face the marshal, now only ten feet away. "I guess I'd better go back in and make my bed."

So quickly that the marshal was taken by surprise, Bump turned from being a bemused giant to a deadly killer. He pulled a gun from under his coat and aimed it at Brink as he pulled the hammer back. But Brink was also quick; he lifted his Colt's Army .44 from its holster, pulling the hammer as he raised the barrel, and got his shot off first.

Marshal Bringham's shot hit Bump in the right shoulder and caused his gun to rise as he pulled the trigger. The shot went just wild enough to miss Brink's head. Brink cocked and fired again, and this shot hit Bump's right arm, causing him to drop the gun and cry out. The marshal cocked his Colt again, but Bump was finally slowed down by pain. Through the smoky haze he looked at Brink with hatred as he tried to stay on his feet. He gave up and sat down heavily on the board-walk. Brink stepped quickly to him and kicked his gun out of reach while he kept his own Colt aimed at the man's head.

The marshal's deputy got up slowly, his own gun in hand now. "You all right, Brink?" he asked.

"Yeah, Bobby. Get me some leg irons."

"Sure thing, Brink." He went into the office and returned in seconds with leg irons, which he fastened around Bump's ankles as the marshal kept his gun ready.

"Now go fetch the doc back here so we can get the holes in this man plugged up."

Bump was still sitting on the boardwalk and holding his right arm. "Pretty good shootin' there, Marshal." He managed to smile thinly.

"I'm afraid you'll be going to jail for more than just a night now, big man." Brink said matter-of-factly.

"You might have to do some repairs first." Bump was cheerful although in pain.

"I can imagine" was Brink's answer.

The doctor came and stopped the bleeding. Brink told the doctor he wanted to get the man into the jail, and then he would let the doctor do whatever else was necessary. The doctor agreed and helped Brink and Bob get Bump into the cell. Brink chained Bump's feet to the bed. Then he and Bob began replacing the bolts that Bump had torn loose from the floor.

From the upstairs hallway window, Nate watched the brief fight outside the jail. He couldn't tell how badly Bump was hurt, but he knew that his plans would have to be altered. If Bump were hurt seriously, which seemed to be the case, he would be of little use; it was the man's immense strength that Nate needed. But he couldn't leave him in custody, where he might trade his knowledge for a lighter sentence. Nate tiptoed down the stairs and slipped down the hall to his room without being seen. He checked his revolver and put it into his pocket. Then he lay down on his bed but didn't close his eyes. He was making a new plan.

Chapter Fourteen

The Pacific Express was late arriving in Chicago. The westbound train to Omaha had already left, but there would be another one the next day. Mary Ann presented her baggage checks in the station, and after about a twenty-minute wait she was in possession of her luggage on the platform. Now she needed to find a carriage to take her to the other train station, where she could leave most of her luggage, and then to a hotel.

At that moment James Whipwell walked up to the side of the platform, leading a string of nine horses. One had a saddle and bridle, and a valise was tied across the saddle.

"Good morning, ma'am," he greeted Mary Ann, and he tipped his hat. "Can I offer you some assistance?" Jimmy could see that the young woman was well-dressed and carried herself with much grace, and he was almost sorry he had approached her. He tried to use what he knew of formal language and hoped he didn't sound like the farm boy he was.

Mary Ann turned to look at the young man who had offered her help. He was taller than average, but not much, dark-haired, clean shaven, well-dressed in wool pants and jacket, with a well-made linen shirt, open at the collar. She had two examples to help her evaluate him: men she remembered from her childhood on the range, and men she had met during her schooling. He seemed to fit neither. His riding boots were clean and shiny, without the wear marks that stirrups and spurs would inevitably leave. He was wearing a gun, unusual in itself in Chicago. The gun was in a holster that hung straight down—not the kind of holster a horseman would wear, yet he was holding a string of horses. He seemed self-assured, but Mary Ann thought that might be attributable to a youthful but subdued brashness, rather than maturity. She thought he might even be younger than she.

She stated what seemed to her to be obvious. "I need a carriage to take my luggage to the other station." Then she realized that the statement had already told him more about herself than she had wanted to reveal.

"You're going on to Council Bluffs, then?" he guessed. "Omaha?" he added, his voice betraying his hope.

She looked around, hoping to see a carriage for hire, before she answered with one word. "Yes". She didn't want to seem either too friendly or too unfriendly. He was an interesting young man, but she was alone and far from home.

Jimmy removed his hat; he wanted to be a perfect gentleman. Then he realized they were still outside, but it was too late. He passed his hat from hand to hand as if it were hot to the touch. "Please allow me to assist you, ma'am. We've missed the train, and we'll have to stay over in Chicago. I would be pleased to help you deliver your luggage to the station."

She looked into his eyes and saw nothing to alarm her. "Very well," she replied, "thank you."

Jimmy found a carriage and loaded her trunks onto the back. Then he gave her a hand into the seat. "I must see to my horses now," he apologized, and he glanced over his shoulder at the string that was nervously waiting. "I've been told that the hotel next to the Union Pacific station is very nice. Would you have dinner with me there tonight?" He was glad that his mother had wanted him to be more than a farm boy and had spent many hours teaching him manners and speech.

She was surprised at how well he spoke, almost as if he had been educated in the East, as she had, or perhaps tutored.

"I don't even know your name," she replied, a slight rebuke.

"James Whipwell," he answered, "and may I know your—?"

"Mary Ann Bringham. It's nice to meet you, Mr. Whipwell."

It took Jimmy a moment to realize that the young woman had the same last name as the marshal who had answered his letter, but he lost that thought as he struggled with what was proper to say next.

"It's my pleasure, Miss Bringham. I'll see you tonight, then?"

She hesitated for just a second. He was going to be on the train tomorrow. There would be ample time to become better acquainted there. "I think not, Mr. Whipwell. I believe I'll retire early tonight. If I don't see you again, may you have a pleasant journey."

"I hope to, ma'am, and may you also," he replied. He wanted to bow but was not sure it was appropriate, so he merely tipped his head forward.

"Good day to you, then." She signaled the driver to leave, and Jimmy stepped back.

During the encounter, neither had smiled.

Jimmy didn't smile often, nor did any of his family. It was not a common Whipwell mannerism.

Mary Ann didn't smile because she was afraid it would be misinterpreted. But as the carriage drove away, the corners of her mouth tilted upward, and she hummed a tune softly.

Jimmy found a stable not far from the Union Pacific station to take care of his horses. He carried his valise back to the hotel and registered. The desk clerk scowled when he saw the holstered revolver at Jimmy's side but said nothing. Chicago was busy and boisterous, but it was not the Wild West that Jimmy was so anxious to experience.

In his room he tried not to think of the young woman he had met at the train station. She had seemed distant and cool, compared to the farm girls he was used to meeting at Saturday dances in Marion. But those girls came to the dances with their families, were watched by their parents at the dance, and always left with their families. This young woman was on her own, he told himself, and she probably preferred to keep it that way. If he could have had a proper introduction in the right setting, she might have warmed to him. He looked forward to the morning, when he hoped he could find her either at the station or on the train and talk with her again.

When the sun got low in the sky, Mary Ann went to the dining room in the hotel for dinner. She was purposely early and sat alone, eating in silence. As she got up to leave, James Whipwell came in to sit down. He saw her and walked over to her, half blocking her exit without really meaning to.

"Miss Bringham." He didn't know what else to say.

"Excuse me, Mr. Whipwell, I'm just leaving." And she made a move to walk on, thinking he would say something that would give her an excuse to pause rather than brush past him. Then they could exchange a few more pleasantries, which was what she wanted. But her bluff worked too well. He clumsily stepped back, embarrassed, and watched her walk out of the dining room and to the stairway. As she climbed the stairs, she wondered why he hadn't said anything more to her. His manners and speech were such that she assumed he had the social skills that would make him comfortable in her presence. She thought it would not be a bad thing for their acquaintanceship to progress, if slowly.

Jimmy watched Mary Ann Bringham go and wondered why she seemed so reluctant to have a conversation with him. He found a seat and ordered a dinner, which was the very first meal he had ever eaten in a well-appointed restaurant. He enjoyed it immensely but then realized that it had cost more than he was used to paying for food in the Marion Café. He could not afford to eat like this again for the present, but someday, he promised himself, it would become a way of life for him.

The next morning Jimmy was up before daybreak and went to the stable to fetch his horses and saddle just as the sun was rising. He paid the hired hand and led the string down the street to the railroad station. There, he found a yard hand, and together they loaded his horses into a stock car. Jimmy then bought some hardtack and biscuits from a station vendor and filled his canteen with water. He boarded the train and sat where he could watch the passenger platform. He hoped to catch a glimpse of Mary Ann.

Mary Ann arose almost as early as Jimmy had and prepared herself for travel. Once she was satisfied with her appearance, she closed her small suitcase and carried it to the lobby, paid her bill, and left. She carried the small suitcase to the station, where she arranged for her trunks to be loaded and sent to her compartment. Jimmy saw her walk across the platform and board the train, but second-class passengers were not allowed into the first-class Pullman car. Disappointed, he settled disconsolately into his seat, and a half hour later the train pulled out of Chicago.

Chapter Fifteen

The doctor stepped back and wiped his hands on a towel. "This arm will never work again, I'm afraid."

Bump looked at the doctor. "I seen a lot worse than this get up and ride horseback in a week. You must not be much of a doc." There was no rancor in his statement, just an observation. He had tolerated the surgery the doctor had performed in the cell without anesthetic and was now watching as his arm was wrapped and braced by padded splints that the doctor had made. He had been shot in his right shoulder and his upper arm by a Colt .44 with as much powder as Marshal Bringham could pack behind a 180-grain slug.

The doctor gathered up bloody gauze from around the bunk before he answered. "You've got two broken bones in your shoulder and a piece of lead in there somewhere that I can't find." He dropped the gauze into a bucket. "Your arm is missing about an inch of bone; I doubt that it will ever heal in a way that it'll be usable," he explained. "But if you want to ride horseback, be my guest." Then he added, "When you get released."

"Well, since I ain't gonna pay you anyway, I guess I got a bargain." Bump gave a wry smile. It was as if the wounds, the probable incapacitation of his dominant arm, and his incarceration meant nothing to him. He was sitting on the edge of his bunk, and his legs were chained to the iron posts. His left hand was free, but his right arm was totally immobilized.

"I'll ask the marshal to bring in an extra mattress, and we'll arrange it so you can sleep sitting up," the doctor informed him. "That's about the best we can do for now."

At the sound of his title, the marshal got up from his desk and walked to the cell to observe. "You about done, Doc?" he asked.

"Yes, Brink. You didn't leave me much to work with, you know." He said it with a little bit of accusation and a little bit of admiration. Bump had told him how quickly Marshal Bringham had pulled his revolver and gotten off the two shots that prevented him from shooting straight. But the doctor wondered how Brink had missed the man's heart at such close range. "You almost missed him, didn't you?" he asked.

Brink shook his head. "No. A man that size can absorb a lot of lead and still kill you. I was aiming for what I hit. I wanted him unable to pull his trigger."

"That was the best shooting I've ever seen, Marshal," Bob said.

The doctor nodded and said, "He may well never pull a trigger again."

"All right with me," Brink answered, and he unlocked the hastily repaired cell so the doctor could exit. The doctor picked up his bag and the bucket of bloody rags, looked once more at the wounded prisoner, and walked out. Brink locked the cell door behind him.

The doctor pulled a chair up to Brink's desk and sat down wearily. "Any coffee left in that pot?" he asked.

"Sure is," Brink answered. He poured the three of them a cup and then sat down in his own chair. No one said anything for a few minutes, which was about how long it took Bump to start snoring.

"What made him take you on, Brink?" the doctor asked.

"I guess he wanted out of Cheyenne. He had a sense of humor right up to the point where he drew his gun." Brink turned to Bob. "He was about to kick your head off when I stopped him."

"He sure took me by surprise, Brink," Bob replied.

"He was in a cell, wasn't he? Where'd he get a gun?" the doctor wanted to know.

"I asked him that," Brink said. "You know what he said? He said someone just poked it through the cell window to him. He said he didn't know who!"

"Do you believe him?"

"No."

"Well, his short-lived break for freedom cost him his right arm, I'm thinking."

The marshal just shrugged.

The doctor changed the subject. "When's your daughter getting in?"

"Saturday."

"What're her plans?"

"I'm hoping she wants to stay out here a while, but I couldn't blame her if she went back to her life in the East. This is not a very good place for a young girl," he said, then corrected himself, "a young woman."

"Cheyenne is going to be a big city one day, Brink," the doctor said. "They've got a brand-new spur to Denver, and there're rumors of gold north of here."

"Well, before that happens, I'd like one or two more deputies."

"Yeah"—the doctor smiled—"and I want a pretty nurse too."

Brink chuckled.

The doctor drank the last of his coffee and stood up.

"It looks like we killed the night, Doc," Brink said.

"That's a fact. I delivered a baby last night—that is, night before last." He shook his head as if to clear it. "I think I'll go home and crawl into bed."

Marshal Bringham patted the doctor on the shoulder and said, "That's a good idea. I'll buy you dinner tonight, all right?"

"You got it."

Both walked to the door. When Brink opened the door, the sun was just coming up along the street, making the dusty whitewash of the storefronts look orange on their eastern side. The doctor tugged on the brim of his hat and walked slowly onto the boardwalk toward home.

The next morning Nate began to make new plans. He wasn't sure how badly Bump was hurt, but he was out of patience with the bigger Hollister. He couldn't leave him alive to tell what he knew about the robbery. There would be no returning to deal with him after the robbery, so he must be killed soon.

Nate knew there were two daily newspapers in Omaha, but they were the last until Cheyenne. The murder of a prisoner in Cheyenne could easily be reported within hours in Omaha, thanks to the telegraph that followed the railroad tracks. He couldn't let Ed Hollister find out that his brother was dead; that would complicate everything far more than just proceeding without Bump. He would not be able to dispose of Bump without risk until he was sure the news would not reach Omaha before Abe and Ed left there. Then, when they arrived, he would tell Ed about Bump's arrest and that he had been unable to secure his release or enable his escape. He wouldn't mention that, by then, he would have silenced Bump.

Nate reviewed what he remembered of the train schedule and recalled that it left Omaha the next morning, Friday, at 11:00. It would travel all day and all night and reach Cheyenne on Saturday morning. Tonight, after the marshal finished his rounds around midnight, Nate knew what he had to do. There would be little chance that the news could reach Omaha before the paper was printed.

Nate needed a horse so that he could ride away from town after killing Bump, rather than driving a mule-drawn wagon, which would make him too conspicuous. The wagon he could park out of sight east of town a few miles and ride out to it. He returned to the livery stable where he had negotiated for a horse and saddle. His money was almost gone, and the horse he was able to purchase was not what he would have liked, but it would have to suffice. He didn't want to rent the horse because he might be forced to ride it a long way, and it would provide more motive for his pursuers. Although he had no intention of returning the wagon and team, he guessed they would be found soon enough and returned to their owner.

He rode his newly acquired mount around to the rear of the hotel and tied it to his wagon. There was nothing more to be done, so he walked into the hotel where he could rest in his room until evening.

Stan Hollister awoke with the sun high in the sky. He had carved himself a den in thick brush along a creek three miles east of Cheyenne. On his way out of town following the train ride, he had managed to steal an apple pie, cooling on a windowsill, and two chickens, but that food was gone now. It was time for him to sneak back into town and see what else he could find to eat. His primitive living conditions bothered him not in the least; most of his adult life had been spent in prison, and he was actually enjoying his freedom and his first experience in the great West. He plunged his head into the creek, drank his fill, and then started toward town.

Marshal Bringham stood in his office after the doctor left and looked into the cell at Bump Hollis. The man was snoring loudly, asleep in a slouch on his bunk, unable to lie down because of his injuries. Brink turned and looked at the wall above his desk, and his gaze fell on the picture of the embezzler from Omaha. He shook his head when he saw the pencil stuck in the picture and the drawn mustache and beard. He had to admire Bump's sense of humor even as he condemned him for the ruthless person he was underneath. He removed the pencil and laid it on his desk as he studied the altered picture.

Was it the skill of the artist that seemed to give the portrait importance, or was it that Brink had recently seen a man of this description? Brink was exhausted; he had slept not at all since the gunfight and was suddenly finding it difficult to keep his eyes open. He decided to find his deputy and turn the town over to him for the day. He touched his badge, lifted his gun once in its holster, let it settle back in lightly, then put his hat on and stepped out the door into the morning.

Chapter Sixteen

The conductor announced the next station, Rock Island, informing the passengers that there would be a ten-minute stop just beyond, at Davenport. They could leave the train there to buy an evening meal, which they would have to eat quickly or bring back on board.

Jimmy went to the end of his car, which coupled with the Pullman car, to watch for Mary Ann. The curtains were pulled to prevent second-class riders from observing the more affluent passengers. He opened the door a crack and saw her get up and walk the opposite direction down the aisle, so when the train stopped at Rockport, he jumped to the platform and quickly walked to the other end of her car, arriving just as she stepped down.

"Miss Bringham," he said, and he lifted his hat.

"Oh, Mr. Whipwell." He had taken her by surprise, but she

had rehearsed what she would say when they met again. "Have you been enjoying the trip?"

"Yes, ma'am. But I'm looking forward to crossing the Missouri, now that we have gained the Mississippi." He had preplanned his opener also.

"Oh, yes, so am I."

"The train will not be here long, and I have a seat to myself. Why not join me in my car, and we can watch the rest of the Mississippi crossing together?"

"Why, yes, that sounds like fun." She took his arm as they walked along the platform to his car. He helped her up into the car and led her to his seat. The whistle blew, and the train began moving.

They sat together and watched all the activity on the mighty Mississippi, and then the train pulled into Davenport. Jimmy helped Mary Ann off the train, and she looked around at the station. "We should get our meal so that we'll have time to eat, away from the train." Jimmy offered his elbow, and she took it, walking with him rapidly across the platform to the station, where a number of tables were set up, and people were sitting and standing around them, eating with gusto. Their conversation was limited by the need to eat rapidly, and when they were finished, they walked quickly back to the train as the conductor announced its departure. Jimmy asked Mary Ann to sit with him again, and she accepted.

"What kind of work do you do, Mr. Whipwell?"

"I'm a horse breeder, but I have also been involved in law enforcement."

"That sounds exciting. I believe I saw you bring your

horses to the train several nights ago. I didn't know what town we were in—it was dark."

"That was Fort Wayne."

"Ah," she said. She wanted to ask him his destination, but she knew that would prompt him to ask hers, and she was not quite ready to offer this information to a man she had just met.

"Do you ride, Miss Bringham?"

"It's been a few years since I've had the opportunity, but I used to," she replied. "I've been attending a university in New York."

"Hmm." Jimmy could not help feeling a little disappointment. He had only home schooling beyond sixth grade and now was more certain than ever that this woman's station was above his own.

Mary Ann sensed his distress. "Please don't think me an eastern society woman," she said. "I spent my childhood in the West."

"Oh," he said, a little flustered. "I didn't think . . ." He didn't know how to finish, so he made a confession of his own. "I've not been west of the Mississippi until now."

"It's wonderful country," she said.

"I have read much about the West, and I'm sure you're right. I'm looking forward to seeing all of it."

She stayed with him until long after dark and well into Iowa, at which point she excused herself and retired to her compartment. Jimmy didn't tell her that his destination was Cheyenne. Because of her last name, he had hoped that her destination was also Cheyenne, but to him, that would have been too good to be true, and he was too unsure of himself to ask her. He assumed that she was bound for some point farther west, and he didn't want to admit to himself or to her that their friendship was destined to be brief. He found out that she had finished her schooling, earning a degree in history, and was returning to her childhood home.

Mary Ann likewise assumed that James was bound for the far west but let herself indulge in the fantasy that somehow they might have more than just a few days together on a train.

Chapter Seventeen

Abe Jackson and Ed Hollister looked over the equipment they had piled on the little table in Abe and Penny's cabin.

"That the only rifle you have?" Ed asked Abe, pointing to a muzzle-loading Springfield.

"Yeah, it's about all I ever need. I shoot a couple deer every year with it." He picked it up and sighted down the barrel at an imaginary deer, made a little explosion sound with his mouth, and said, "Got 'im!" Then he laid the rifle down, grinning.

"You'd better get a repeater somewhere. This won't be any deer hunt," Ed Hollister growled.

"I got a pistol, a Remington Army .44, that'll be good enough," Abe argued.

"You get out and buy yourself a rifle."

"Shoot, I just barely got enough left for my ticket now."

"Borrow one. Steal one."

"Aw, I don't want—"

Ed dropped something onto the table loudly and took a step back. "You get a rifle, or I'll wire Bump to come on back, and we'll find our own job! I'm not going in on a fool's operation!" he stated forcefully. What was actually going through his mind was that he should kill this easygoing, small-time, slow-thinking man and carry on without him. Naturally, he would have to kill Penny too, but that gave him no pause.

"I'll figure something out," Abe said lamely.

Ed wasn't mollified. He stood angrily across the table from Abe without moving, veins in his forehead pulsing.

Abe shuffled his feet and turned to Penny, who was sitting nearby, watching with poorly masked disapproval.

"Penny, how about giving me that old Colt's Navy of your pa's? I can prob'ly trade it for a Henry, or at least a Spencer."

Penny started to lie and tell him that it had too much sentimental value, but she was afraid he would try to take it anyway, and then, when he discovered it missing, he would have more questions. "I sold it" was all she said.

"By dang, Penny, I need a rifle! That woulda got me one. Why'd you sell it?"

"I needed money." She looked away. She knew he had no idea of their finances and would not be aware of the difference that selling a pistol would make.

"Dang, woman, I'm trying to do something for us and you're . . ." He let his comment die. He knew she was on the verge of walking out on him, and he couldn't bear that thought. She had been as faithful to him as a dance hall girl could be, had been his main support, covered his gambling debts, fed him, paid the rent on the little cabin where they lived, and loved him with passion. He knew he would never do better, and in any case he was as devoted to her as she was to him. He looked at her with apology in his eyes, and she looked back at him with her "don't go" expression. He turned back to Ed and said, "I'll borrow a shotgun from Lance at the harness shop. He owes me for some cowhide I brought in." He looked at Ed for a sign of approval but got none. "That'll be handier than a rifle, anyway."

"Yeah, I guess," Ed growled. He wished he and Bump weren't split up. This job was not feeling right to him, but, in spite of his threat to send a telegram to Bump, there was really no way to back out without putting Bump at risk. He had correctly appraised Nate Jackson as ruthless and had warned Bump to be careful when he left. The promised profit of eight thousand dollars was enough incentive to keep him in the plan, but he began to think of charting his own course through the next few days. He resolved that once they got on the train, he would dispose of Abe at the first sign of a problem and carry on by himself. He could tell Abe's brother that Abe fell off the train or, more credibly, that Abe lost interest and stayed in Omaha with Penny. He stepped back to the table. They still had work to do, and they had to catch the train in the morning.

"We need more rope," Ed stated.

"I got more in the trap shed. I'll go get it." Abe went to the door, thankful that Ed was calming down.

"Do you have a big hammer and a cold chisel?" Ed asked. His emotions were almost back to normal.

"I got two hammers. I'll bring 'em both. And a chisel." He left.

Penny sat very still for several minutes. She hated being alone with this man who was more mean-spirited than any man she had known. As much as she disliked Nate Jackson, she thought Ed Hollister was worse. At least Nate could act like a gentleman when he had to; Ed Hollister, in her estimation, was no better than an animal. Her hand was clenched on the little gun that Jacko had given her, concealed in the folds of her dress. She maintained her silence until she heard Abe's footsteps coming back. When she knew she would be safe in a matter of seconds, she quietly said, "If you let harm come to Abe, I'll have no trouble convincing some of the men I know to hunt you down and cut your throat." Her gaze never wavered, and she didn't blink.

Ed's eyes got wide, then narrow, and the veins in his forehead jumped out once more, but before he could form a reply, Abe entered the cabin. He dropped two coils of rope, a hammer, a hatchet, and a chisel onto the table. "I thought we could use the hatchet too," he declared.

Ed glared at Penny for another few seconds, took a deep breath and, turning to Abe, said, "I brought a bag that'll carry most of this stuff. We'll wrap it in a blanket so it won't rattle, and that'll be your luggage on the train."

Abe sensed that something was wrong and glanced from Ed to Penny and back, then said, "Yeah, all right." He couldn't figure out what was up. He pulled a blanket from his bed, and they began wrapping the tools and rope.

When they had assembled and packed all the tools Nate had told them to bring, Abe sat down heavily. Penny was standing next to the stove, and Ed Hollister stood next to the door.

Abe said, "I ain't never been more'n a few miles west of here. I reckon I'll see some new country tomorrow for sure. Penny, are you going to see me off at the train station?"

"No," Penny answered.

Ed asked, "Do you still have the money for the tickets?"

"I already got the tickets. Penny's been taking care of 'em. Penny?"

Penny went to the bed and pulled an envelope from under the mattress. She handed it to Abe silently.

"I'll take mine now," Ed said, and he held out a hand.

Abe relinquished one of the tickets.

"Don't forget the equipment," Ed said, "and don't forget to get a rifle or a shotgun." Then he opened the door and walked out.

Penny had resigned herself to Abe's participation in the scheme, and she spoke no more about it that evening. That night, in bed, she wanted him to hold her, but he didn't, and she wouldn't let herself wrap her arms around him. She lay very still, close enough to feel his warmth but not touching. It took her hours to fall asleep.

Chapter Eighteen

Thursday evening, as promised, the marshal and the doctor had a pleasant meal together in the café. Each had slept the day away. There had been no medical emergencies for the doctor, and Bob, Brink's deputy, had kept the town quiet. The marshal would take over as soon as he and the doctor had finished their supper and talked themselves out.

The conversation was dominated by Marshal Bringham's anticipation of seeing his daughter for the first time in years. The doctor patiently let Brink go on and on about how intelligent she was, how beautiful she was, how much she looked like her mother, and other fatherly brags. At length they both pushed back from the table in the restaurant, which was now almost empty of customers, bid each other good night, and went their respective ways.

On his way to his office, Brink found Bob walking his rounds.

"Everything under control, Bob?" he asked.

"Yeah, Marshal. I think the town has had enough excitement for a few days."

"How's Bump doing?"

"He won forty matches at poker. He thinks he's on top of the world." Bob laughed, and so did the marshal. Bump Hollis was certainly a most unusual character.

"Tell you what, Bob, the café is still open. Get on over there and tell them your dinner is on me, all right?"

"You got it, Marshal. Put my shotgun back in the rack?" He handed it over.

"No problem. See you in the morning."

Brink sat at his desk and began cleaning his pistol. He had not attended to it since the shootout with Bump. He removed the cylinder, flipped the caps off, and unscrewed the nipples. He poured the powder onto a sheet of paper, folded the paper, and poured the powder into a flask. Then he forced the lead out forward and put the projectiles into a glass jar to be melted and remolded later. He disassembled the rest of the weapon and diligently cleaned all the powder residue from the parts. A careful shooter could make a black-powder weapon last for years, even decades, in spite of regular use, but if one chose not to clean his weapon after every use, it could be eaten by corrosion and become useless in a matter of months. When he was done, he carefully reloaded it.

*   *   *

Nate reined the team to a stop in a grove of trees about four miles east of Cheyenne. His saddled horse was tied to the back of the wagon. He climbed into the wagon bed to see if his recent purchases were all there. Black powder, fuse, shovels, picks, pry bars, two cans of coal oil, two lanterns, and various other tools were all there. He pulled a shotgun from under the seat, jumped down from the wagon, and tied the team to a tree, leaving them in harness. Then he mounted the horse and rode into the orange sky toward Cheyenne. He had a date with Bump, and it was not going to be a pleasure for Hollister.

"You got a Mr. Hollis registered here?" Stan asked the desk clerk.

"Yes, sir, but he's not in his room."

"Got any idea where I can find him?"

"Over to the jail. He got into a little trouble." Leo watched the stranger's face closely to gauge his reaction to the news. Strangely, he thought he saw the man smile ever so slightly.

"That'd be about right, I reckon."

Leo was briefly tempted to tell this stranger that Bump had been seriously wounded but decided he would be wise to mind his own business. The man seemed in good spirits, and something about his manner told Leo to leave well enough alone.

Stan walked out of the hotel. He had surveyed the town and already knew where the jail was. He found a vantage point where he could watch the activity around the jail, unseen, and assess his chances of breaking Bump out.

* * *

It was late when Marshal Bringham got up from his desk to make rounds. He strapped on his gun, pinned his badge onto his jacket, and looked at the pictures tacked to the wall above his desk. He had received another picture of the bank embezzler who was now wanted for murder, and he tacked that to the wall next to the first one. This picture was different, but it looked equally familiar. As he closed his eyes for a moment, it struck him. This was the man he had met days ago in the hardware store!

The marshal stepped out onto the boardwalk, lifting his gun slightly in its leather and touching his badge. It was dark on the streets now, with just the glow from the boardwalk lamps. Brink paused in front of his office to let his eyes adjust to the dark. He looked both ways along the main street for the wagon but saw only horses. Maybe the man had left town. Brink cursed at the thought that he had let a murderer come into his town and leave without capturing him. He would check the alley behind the hotel first; the wagon had been tied there yesterday.

Nate stopped on the road just outside of Cheyenne. He was clever; if he rode right up to the jail and shot Bump in his cell, he would have to ride away fast, attracting attention. He would surely be followed and might not be able to elude his pursuers on his way back to the wagon. He decided to leave his horse in the alley a block from the jail. After killing Bump, he would melt into the crowd of curiosity-seekers that would inevitably gather. Then, he could walk innocently to his horse and ride away to keep his rendezvous with the westbound train.

Marshal Bringham looked down the alley behind the hotel and then walked around to the front, where he entered and hailed the desk clerk. "Leo," he asked, "has the man with the wagon checked out?"

"Yes, sir. About three this afternoon, I think." He turned the register around to read it. "Yes, about three."

Brink swore under his breath. It was too dark to try to track the wagon. A murderer had been right under his nose and was now gone.

"Something else, Marshal."

"What's that, Leo?"

"A stranger was here earlier, asking about that man you arrested—Hollis."

"Bump?"

"Yeah, I guess. He only used his first initial and last name when he registered."

At that moment two loud blasts sounded from the direction of the jail. Brink drew his revolver and rushed into the street, looking both ways. All he saw were people running toward the jail. He refrained from running into the street but kept his vantage point on the boardwalk, watching where people were running. Young men were running toward the jail, and old men were walking away; there were few women on the street. He recognized everyone he saw, so he descended the few steps to the street, holstered his gun, and began walking toward the jail.

In the jail Brink turned the lamp up and was confronted with as gory a scene as he had seen in his career as a law-man. Bump was laid out on the floor of his cell, and there was not a square inch of his body that was not bloody. Blood was spattered on the walls and floor of the cell and even out into the office. Bump's eyes were open, and he was trying to speak, but his mouth was full of blood.

"Who did this, Bump?" Brink asked, leaning over, but Bump only stared at the ceiling and moved his lips without making a sound other than gurgling. "Do you know who did this?" Brink thought that Bump tried to nod his head. Brink sent for the doctor and then, pocketing the cell door keys and grabbing the lamp, walked out and around to the back of the jail in the alley. There were footprints everywhere, and Brink could make no sense of them, but under the window of Bump's cell was a wooden box. It was obvious that someone had stood on the box in order to get a better line of sight into the cell. Brink went back into the office, and only seconds behind him was the doctor.

"Oh, my God!" the doctor muttered as Brink let him into the cell. He went immediately to work, trying to sponge blood out of Bump's mouth to let him breathe better. Then he began cutting Bump's clothes off. The marshal lit every lamp he had and carried them into the cell

Brink's deputy entered the office at that time and, glanc-ing into the cell briefly, turned to Brink.

"What in the world happened, Brink?"

"Somebody poked a shotgun through the bars from the al-ley and let both barrels go."

"Are you hit?"

"No, I was at the hotel, looking for the man on that latest flyer."

"No one saw who did this?"

"No, but come here." Brink pointed to the poster of Nate. "I don't know if this guy had anything to do with it, but he's a murderer, and he was right here in town until this afternoon."

"Dang, Brink."

Brink left Bob to guard the doctor and his patient while he deputized a few men he knew he could trust. They all got horses and rode around the perimeter of town in pairs, carrying lanterns.

After pulling the trigger on both barrels of his shotgun, Nate inserted the gun into one pant leg to the knee, tucking the stock under his arm. Then he walked calmly between two buildings on the other side of the alley to another street and circled back. When he arrived back on Main Street, there were people running and shouting. Just before he stepped into the light, he spied the marshal crossing the street from the direction of the hotel. He quickly stepped back into the shadows between two buildings and waited until the marshal had entered the jail. Then he walked right down the boardwalk toward the jail, peered in to see the Marshal looking down at Bump on the floor, and walked on by. In minutes he was on his horse and riding leisurely out of town along the railroad tracks to his wagon. He saw Brink's men with the lanterns and had no difficulty avoiding them.

From his vantage point, Stan Hollister had witnessed the entire incident. When Nate Jackson had pushed the barrel of the shotgun through the cell window, Stan had thought it was part of a jailbreak effort. When the gun fired both barrels and then the shooter calmly hid the gun in his clothing and walked out into the street, Stan knew that he and his brothers had been betrayed. He also knew it would be a miracle if Bump had survived the blast. With difficulty he restrained himself from gunning Nate Jackson down in the street and instead followed him as he made his circuitous way out of town.

An hour later Brink called off the search for the shooter, thanked the men for their service, and returned to the jail. The doctor was still working on Bump, who was alive but breathing very shallowly. Brink was amazed that the man was still alive and looked at the doctor with the obvious question in his eyes.

"He gonna make it, Doc?"

The doctor shook his head but continued working.

"I'll get you some help. Stay here with the doc, Bob." Brink left to find help.

He went directly to the rooming house, where he knew that his former prisoner, April, was staying. He had to awaken the owner to take him to April's room, where he tapped on the door. In a minute a small voice asked through the door, "Who is it?"

"It's the marshal, April. I need your help."

Without hesitation she answered, "I'll be right out. Wait there."

In a few minutes the door opened, and April came out with a question on her face. The marshal responded, "I have a prisoner who has been wounded, and the doctor needs help. Are you afraid of blood?"

"No," she answered.

At the jail, the marshal introduced April to the doctor, and in minutes she was working beside him. The doctor looked at Brink and nodded his approval. Brink watched the two of them as they worked as quickly as they could to remove the lead pellets and stop the bleeding.

Bump was not bleeding profusely from any one wound; he was bleeding from many wounds, from his neck down to his mid-thigh. The shotgun used on him would have been worthless for hunting but deadly when used as it was. The shooter had stood on a wooden box and poked the shotgun through the bars in the window. Bump had backed up as far as he could, but there was no escape.

It would be another long night for the doctor, unless, of course, Bump died soon, which was not unlikely.

Chapter Nineteen

Hours later and miles to the west, Abe Jackson slipped out of bed, kissed his sleeping sweetheart good-bye, shouldered his bag, and left the cabin. He walked to the harness shop, where he tried to convince Lance, the owner, that the few cowhides he had salvaged from winter kill were worth a double-barreled shotgun. He had seven dollars over what his ticket would cost, and in the end he had to give that to Lance, along with his Remington .44, for the shotgun and ammunition. He wouldn't have a belt gun at all. He disassembled the shotgun and packed it in the bag with the tools.

As soon as Abe left the cabin, Penny sprang from bed. She stood before her mirror and cut her long, curly hair short. She dressed herself in an old pair of Abe's pants and shirt, then cut the sleeves from one of her shirts, making it a vest, and put that on over Abe's shirt, the better to hide her breasts. The jacket, for which she had traded her father's revolver, was too big, but it was in keeping with the rest of her clothes, giving her a shabby, needy appearance. The hat had a wide brim, and she would be able to use it to hide her face, which was too delicate to belong to a working man. She put the two-shot derringer into one of the coat pockets, then noticed that it showed through the threadbare fabric of the pocket, so she removed it and put it into her pants pocket. Better.

Fastened to the bottom of a drawer in her dresser was an envelope. She tore it loose and removed forty-one dollars in bills. It would be more than enough to buy a ticket, leaving enough for food for quite a while if she were careful. She pushed the money into her shirt pocket and buttoned the flap over it. She also selected some jewelry from her small collection and added it to the shirt pocket.

She had no suitcase, but Abe had a pair of saddlebags hanging on the wall, although he had no saddle or horse. She took them down and stuffed them with as many of her belongings as she could, and then she, too, left the cabin.

She had no plan other than to be on the train to protect Abe and, if things started going bad, to extricate him and herself. Somehow.

That same morning in Cheyenne, Marshal Bringham awoke after getting almost no sleep for the second night in a row. Bump Hollis was still alive, attended by April while the doctor, also without sleep for a second night, dozed in the marshal's office. Brink walked wearily to the telegraph office to verify that the westbound was on time.

"Yes, sir, Marshal, they left Des Moines at 1:04 this morning; that'll leave them only seven minutes late."

"Very good, Paul. No problems on the rest of the track that you know of?"

"No, sir. They tell me the Missouri River is a little high for this time of year, so the ferry crossing will be easy. I look for them to leave Omaha right on time."

"Thanks, Paul. How's your family?"

"Everyone's happy and healthy, Marshal."

"That's good to hear, Paul. Tell Martha hello for me."

"I'll do that, Marshal. Tell me, what do you hear from your daughter?"

Marshal Bringham couldn't suppress a smile as he answered, "She's on the westbound, Paul. I'm looking forward to seeing her." That was an understatement.

Now Paul knew why the marshal was interested in the westbound. "Well, of course, Marshal. What a happy time for you. Tell you what, I'll send you word if the train has any delays. Otherwise, she should be here tomorrow morning at nine sharp. Your daughter, that is."

"Thanks, Paul. Hopefully we can have you and Elizabeth over for dinner after Mary Ann gets settled."

"That would be very enjoyable, Brink. We'll count on it."

Marshal Bringham knocked twice on the counter, raised his hand in a simple wave, and left the telegraph office.

* * *

The train pulled into Council Bluffs ten minutes behind time. The conductor reset his watch to agree with the clock on top of the train station. This was a familiar ritual; each town kept its own time, usually setting their main clock, wherever that might be, according to the sun's position in the sky.

Jimmy had arranged to meet Mary Ann this morning and help her transfer her trunks to the Missouri River ferry and, after crossing the river, to the Omaha railroad station. He unloaded his horses, threw his saddle onto his own horse, and then led them to Mary Ann's car. When she disembarked, they walked together to the omnibus that would take them to the ferry. Jimmy tied his string of horses behind. At the freight car were several wagons to transfer the westbound freight to the other side of the river. The same was true at the baggage car. Mary Ann swiveled around as they passed, hoping to get a view of her luggage as they passed but was unable to.

As the omnibus descended the muddy riverbank, it slid to one side, and Mary Ann grabbed Jimmy's arm to keep herself steady. When she relaxed a little as the omnibus rolled straight ahead, she let go of his arm and looked at his face. He returned the look, and, when the omnibus had to negotiate a rough part of the route, he wrapped one arm around her shoulders and gripped the rail tightly with the other. She looked at him with approval.

Owing to the level of the water, the omnibus and the freight wagons were able to cross a makeshift wooden ramp to the ferry without having to descend the steeper part of the muddy banks.

The ferry was just a large floating platform where live-stock, baggage, and freight were all stacked in random piles. Jimmy lifted Mary Ann out of the omnibus and stepped through the mud to deposit her on the ferry.

"Oh, my!" she said. "Thank you, James." She touched his arm, and he bowed slightly and then retrieved his horses, en-couraging them as they boarded the ferry.

As soon as everything was loaded, the ferry made its way across the Missouri and tied up on the west side. As the om-nibus driver negotiated the ramp and urged his team up the gentler part of the muddy west bank, Jimmy wondered how difficult it would be if the water were lower. Again he held tightly to Mary Ann. The omnibus gained the road, which was only marginally better than the riverbank, and made its way into Omaha and the Union Pacific railroad station. Jimmy was eager to see his horses loaded safely into a stock car, so he jumped out of the omnibus and helped Mary Ann down. Then he excused himself to Mary Ann and went to his horses.

At the stock car, he waited with another man who was leading two saddled horses. The man was not dressed well, but Jimmy scarily noticed. What he did notice was that one of the horses was quite old and would surely not carry a man very far, while another seemed to limp, and the same could be said of it. If this was what the West had to offer, Jimmy told himself, he would make a fortune by breeding superior animals.

It only took minutes with the other man's help to load all the horses. Jimmy's stallion had been saddled for the conve-nience of transferring the saddle across the river. Inside the car was a railing to hold saddles. Jimmy removed the saddle and tied it to the rail and then helped the other man by removing one of his saddles and placing it next to his. Jimmy couldn't help but notice that the saddles were in as poor shape as the horses, but he said nothing except, "You're welcome," when the man thanked him for his help. That done, he walked to his own car, boarded the train, and put his valise on a seat.

Because the train was not due to leave for almost an hour, he found Mary Ann, and they shared a late breakfast in a shabby little café not far from the train station. She had been watching when he loaded his horses.

"I think your horses are quite beautiful, James," she said.

"Oh. Well, I . . ." Jimmy was flustered. "I guess I never thought of them in that way."

"Oh, but they are!" she said.

"Well, thank you. They're the result of twenty-five years of breeding."

Mary Ann raised her eyebrows. She was sure Jimmy was not nearly that old.

"My mother had a mare that was one of the best horses ever," he explained. "She bred it several times to provide horses for our farm. When I was born, she reserved a stallion for me. When I was young, I would ride my stallion to other farms and breed their mares. Sometimes I was allowed to keep a foal. I started trading horses before I was ten, with my mother's help, and all but two of my horses are descendants of my mother's mare."

"That's a wonderful story, James."

Jimmy flushed. "Thank you. I'm quite proud of my horses."

"And I'm sure your mother is equally proud of you."

Jimmy's face clouded. "She passed away five years ago."

"Oh. I'm so sorry to hear that." Mary Ann reached across the table and put her hand on his. He hoped she didn't hear him inhale sharply in surprise.

Ed Hollister and Abe Jackson boarded the train separately, as per Nate's instructions. Ed got directly on, leaving the loading of the horses to Abe. They sat in the same car, however, where they could keep an eye on each other. Abe had Nate's written plan in his pocket, unknown to Ed. He knew that sometime in the early hours of the next morning they would reach the point where Nate and Bump would have disrupted the train tracks in some manner. Abe even knew where that point would be—east of Cheyenne about thirty-five miles. Just before that was due to happen, he and Ed would disarm the men in each car and block the doors shut with nails or rope. Anyone who looked like a troublemaker would be tied up. Nate had told Abe to help himself to any money or valuables he could take from the passengers, and that would increase their profit. Abe hoped he would find a lady passenger with fancy jewelry, and he could take it to Penny to make amends. He had spotted several women who looked well-to-do.

Penny slouched on a barrel on the freight platform with her hat pulled low and watched the train. She saw a young man load a string of horses at the same time that Abe loaded his two. She watched as other passengers struggled with their own luggage. She saw Abe and Ed Hollister board at opposite ends of a car, and then she ambled to the station platform and positioned herself to see which car they sat down in. When she was sure which car they were in, she boarded the train two cars away.

Mary Ann had gone to her seat in the Pullman car to get settled, and Jimmy was sitting alone near the end of his car, as close as possible to her car, waiting for the train to start. He didn't pay much attention to the man who came down the aisle and sat next to him.

Then the man spoke. "Howdy."

Jimmy turned from looking out the window and smiled at the man. It was the man with the two horses. "Hello," he said. "My name is James Whipwell."

"Mine's Abe. Jackson," he added. "Mighty pleased. You goin' far?"

"Well, actually I've been on the train since Fort Wayne—two days. I'm getting off at Cheyenne. How about you?"

"Well, I got no definite plans," Abe lied. "Shoot, I'm just gonna ride 'til I reach a place that looks purty good to me." And that place should be thirty-five miles east of Cheyenne, if Nate had done his job.

Jimmy looked at the man. He was somewhere between thirty and forty, dressed like a working man, wearing a soiled cap and not carrying a gun. His face was creased with wrinkles, and he was missing part of a tooth, but that seemed not to discourage him from smiling broadly.

"There's a lot of country ahead of us. I'm sure you'll have success," Jimmy said.

"Well, thank ya, James. I jest never worry about it too much." He grinned again.

"Call me Jimmy, Abe." He offered his hand, which Abe took. Jimmy liked this man; he was warm, congenial, and full of humor. And they seemed to have several things in common.

"Ya got it, Jimmy." Soon they were engrossed in conversation about railroads, Indians, rivers, farms, horses—Abe seemed to have experience at almost everything and a good-natured opinion to match. Jimmy forgot about Mary Ann for the moment.

At the other end of the car, Ed Hollister was not as happy. He had never been able to make friends easily, and he couldn't convince himself that Abe and James Whipwell were strangers who just happened to find something in common to talk about. Whipwell was dressed like a sheriff or marshal and was wearing a gun. His face might be youthful, but Ed was convinced that Whipwell was a traveling lawman or, worse, a railroad detective. And that idiot Abe was talking to him freely!

Just before Lincoln, Mary Ann left her Pullman car to find Jimmy, hoping to eat with him. When she looked through the doorway of his car, she could see Jimmy, Abe, and several other men in a cluster, telling stories, laughing, and smoking cigars. She decided she wasn't hungry and returned to her seat. She told herself that she had no reason to expect that

James Whipwell would make all his time available to her. And she certainly wouldn't make all hers available to him, either.

From the other end of the train, Penny strolled to the car where Abe and his new friends were conversing. She watched him for a moment, then her eyes searched for Ed Hollister and found him at the end of the car, his back to her as he glared at the jovial group of travelers gathered around Abe and the well-dressed man. One of the men had produced a bottle of whiskey and was sharing it with the others. Penny watched and then strolled back to her seat. She had a small problem: there was only a women's restroom on the train; men traveling second class were expected to use the platform on the last car. She would have to get off the train and run for a bush at most stops and try not to attract attention.

When the conductor announced Grand Island, Mary Ann again came out to see if Jimmy wanted to eat with her. The group had broken up, and several of the men were slouched in their seats, asleep and snoring. Abe was one of the sleepers, but Jimmy, who had only sampled the whiskey—his first drink of alcohol—was awake and smiled when he saw her enter his car. He joined her at the Grand Island station for dinner, which they had to bolt down, and then they sat together in his car as they had the night before until well past dark. They were still together when the train stopped at Kearney and again when it stopped at North Platte at about midnight.

"I should get back to my car, James."

"I didn't mean to keep you from your rest. You've been

traveling many days longer than I have. You must be exhausted."

"Oh, not at all. Our conversations have made the trip much more pleasant." She looked into his eyes to make sure that he was interpreting this in the most intimate way, and she knew immediately that he was.

"I haven't asked you your destination, but I must tell you that I'll be leaving the train at Cheyenne," he said with regret.

"Oh, my goodness! So will I!" She placed a hand on his arm, and his regret turned to elation.

"That's wonderful!" he said. Then he remembered her last name. "Tell me, are you by any chance related to the marshal in Cheyenne?"

"Yes, he's my father." She smiled. "Do you know him?"

"We have corresponded in the matter of my employment by him." He was quick to add, "He made me no promises, but I feel confident that when we meet, I can persuade him to hire me."

"He will." She was still smiling. "He and I like many of the same things."

This was not lost on Jimmy.

It felt impossible for Mary Ann to leave Jimmy for the comfort of her compartment. She stayed another hour while they talked in much more detail about themselves, sharing more information than they had been willing to share when they thought they might never see each other again. Mary Ann, in her excitement, took Jimmy's hand in hers so often that finally he held it tightly and didn't let it go.

Chapter Twenty

The next stop after North Platte was O'Fallon's. There would be no passengers; the engine would take on water and wood. Abe became restless as the loading was noisily accomplished, but when the train pulled out, the whistle awakened him. He sat up and watched out the window for a long time, but the darkness hid everything. He arose and clumsily made his way to the last car on the train, where he went to the rear platform to relieve himself. He walked right past Penny without recognizing her, partly because she, also awakened by the whistle, saw him coming and hid her eyes under the brim of her hat. A minute later Ed Hollister followed Abe's path to the rear of the train, and Penny saw him and reasoned that he and Abe were going someplace where they could discuss their plan in private. Five minutes later Ed returned, and Penny watched his back as he continued up the aisle away

149

from her. She was trying with everything she possessed to will him to drop dead right there in the middle of the aisle. She even briefly considered pulling her derringer and shooting him in the back, then throwing the gun out the window. Almost everyone was asleep, the car was almost dark, and she thought there was a good chance she could get away with it.

Fifteen minutes went by, and still Abe had not returned from the rear platform. Penny felt strangely uneasy. What was taking him so long? Women riding trains knew not to blunder out onto the rear platform on the last car, but she was dressed as a man; no one would pay her any attention. She still didn't want Abe to know she was on the train, but she could approach the door and try to get a glimpse of him. She had a feeling that something was not right.

Penny got to the last row of seats and could see no one on the rear platform through the glass in the door. She looked over her shoulder. The aisle was empty, and she quietly walked to the door and pressed her face to the window, looking both left and right. Her heart sank; the platform was empty!

Penny whirled around angrily and for just a moment was going to charge right up the aisle and kill Ed Hollister. Then she got control of herself and started thinking. Maybe Abe was on top of the train, going forward to disable the engineer. No, that didn't seem likely; he could just walk up the aisle and then climb over the tender in front of the first car. Or was there a freight car in the way? She couldn't remember what the train had looked like in Omaha. It seemed Abe would still have gone as far as possible inside the train before taking on the dangerous task of climbing over the top.

Who was the young man Abe had been sitting with? He was well dressed without being fancy; was he a railroad detective? Could he help her? No, she wouldn't involve a stranger yet. She walked forward to Abe's car.

The first seat she passed was the one in which Ed Hollister had been sitting. It was empty. She looked over the rest of the car from where she was standing and saw that everyone was slouched down or curled up on the seats, trying to sleep on the noisy, pitching, rolling passenger car as it sped through Nebraska. She slowly walked forward until she came to the seat where Abe had been sitting. His jacket was wadded up next to the window, where he had been using it as a pillow. He wouldn't have gone outside for very long without his jacket. She knew he didn't have the fare for a Pullman car, but those were the only cars left on the train that she hadn't searched. She picked up his jacket, felt the pockets, and found his ticket stub, his tobacco, and nothing else.

A voice in the semidarkness spoke with quiet authority. "Drop the jacket, and let me see your hands, mister!" Caught by surprise, she hesitated and then heard a gun hammer click back. "Do it now, mister!" She did as she was told.

"What do you think you're doing there, mister?" the voice asked.

She looked up and saw the man who had been sitting with Abe earlier. She answered with a question of her own but forgot, in the moment, to lower her voice. "Where is the man who was wearing this jacket?"

Jimmy's eyes narrowed. This stranger in baggy clothes sounded like a boy but moved like . . . like a woman. While he kept his gun level, he lifted the brim of her hat. It *was* a woman. He slowly lowered the hammer on his revolver. The train began slowing, as it had periodically, to take on water.

"Who are *you*?" Jimmy asked.

Although he had lowered the hammer, he held his revolver pointed in her direction. He felt like a law officer, his jurisdiction this passenger car, and it looked as if he had caught a robber in the act. He made up his mind that everything he did must be exactly correct. There was a flicker of an image in his mind of his accepting the thanks of the grateful railroad, but he snapped his mind back to the present. No time for daydreaming.

"I need help," Penny said. "This is my husband's jacket, and I can't find him on the train."

Abe was not Penny's husband, but Penny thought of him in that way and referred to him as such when talking to strangers.

This was starting to sound like something other than a robbery. Jimmy replaced his revolver back in its holster. "What's going on here?" It didn't make sense to him that this woman, disguised as a man, would ride a train in a separate car from her husband.

The train slowed to a stop at the water tower. Penny braced herself against a seat back. "My husband is going west to find work. I quit my job to follow him, but I . . . I didn't want him to see me yet." That was nearly the truth, but it raised more questions than it answered. Before Jimmy could say anything, she went on, "Something has happened to him. Help me, please."

"Who is your husband?"

"He's the man you were sitting with earlier, Abe Jackson. Please!" she begged.

Now Jimmy recognized the jacket. He was angry with himself for not recognizing it instantly; after all, he had sat and talked with the man for hours. A nice guy, seemingly. Now he was in trouble, and Jimmy was being asked to help. He looked at Penny and thought she was about to cry. He wanted to question her further, but he had the feeling that time was not on their side. "Let's find the conductor," he said.

Chapter Twenty-one

Marshal Bringham was catching a nap in his office after making rounds following supper. His intent was to awaken at nine and make rounds once more before retiring for the night, but he was too tired to wake up at the command of his usually reliable internal clock. Bump Hollis was still in his cell, being too heavy to move, where he was in very serious condition. April was sitting up with the man enjoying her new status as nursemaid and doctor's assistant. The marshal had a home but wanted to establish an official presence around the clock in his office in the wake of the unsolved assault on his prisoner. He was also there to protect April, should the killer return.

"Marshal, wake up, it's Paul. I need to talk to you." The voice seemed very far away.

Marshal Bringham sat up and rubbed his eyes. He had left

a lamp on low and now used that light to look at his watch: 10:00 P.M. He looked around to see if April was all right, and seeing her produced the thought in his sleep-fogged mind that he would see his daughter in twelve hours. He was about to fall asleep again when he realized that someone was pounding on the door and calling his name. April got up from her chair and came to the marshal, gently touching his shoulder.

"Marshal," she said softly.

He stood up, rubbed his eyes, and then adjusted the flame on his lamp.

"Marshal, there's someone at the door."

Brink went to the door, looked through the peephole to identify the visitor, and then opened it. It was Paul from the telegraph office.

"Marshal, the telegraph line is down between here and Sidney."

"What does that mean, Paul?"

"Well, it could mean Indian trouble, but they don't usually do things like that at night. Besides, the trains have reported few Indians in that area."

"How do you know it's between here and Sidney?" the marshal asked.

"I can wire North Platte through Denver, and they can reach Sidney, but I can't wire them directly."

"Do you mean to tell me that there's someone in the offices of those little stops at night?"

"When the train is coming, yes, in some of them—to coordinate the eastbound and the westbound."

"I see. What about the weather?"

"Calm for this time of year."

"What do you think happened?" the marshal asked.

"It's only two wires, each about the size of a pencil lead, a hundred miles long. It could be anything." Paul shrugged. "I just wanted you to know."

"Very well. Are you going to keep trying to raise them?"

"Definitely. All the operators on this part of the line are on alert, on the off chance it's something serious."

"Very well. I'll make rounds and then stop by your office before I call it a night."

"All right, Marshal. I'll be there." Paul returned to the telegraph office.

The marshal walked to the cell where Bump was lying unconscious. "Has he said anything, April?"

"No, sir."

"Are you all right?"

"Yes."

The marshal left to walk through the town. The gunfight in the dance hall Wednesday night and the shooting of Bump in the jail Thursday night had had a sobering effect on the nightlife of Cheyenne. There were no signs of trouble in any of the saloons, and so, at midnight, as he had promised, he went to the telegraph office. There was a light on inside, and Paul was sitting at the telegrapher's desk. Brink tapped twice on the door and walked in.

"Hello, Marshal."

"Any change in the line?"

Paul looked at the clock on the wall. "No," he said, "not as of seven minutes ago."

"All right, then. I'll be in my office. I need to get a few more hours of sleep."

"If you don't mind my saying so, Marshal, you look as if you could use it."

"That's true. Good night, Paul. Don't hesitate to wake me if there's any change."

"Sure, Marshal. Sleep well."

Brink walked back to his office and fell asleep almost immediately.

April watched as he did so and realized that the marshal was nearing his limit. She wished there was something she could do for him, but she couldn't think what it might be. Her father had died in the war, and that was when she began leading the life that had brought her to Cheyenne. Marshal Bringham reminded her of her father a little.

In his cell, Bump took a huge breath, exhaled long and noisily, and breathed no more. April jumped up from her chair and looked at his face. She had been reaching through the bars, taking his pulse all day, and it had been getting harder and harder to find. This time she couldn't find it at all. When she was convinced that he was dead, she sat back in her chair and closed her eyes. She was sure, from what the marshal had told her, that Bump was a very bad man, but she took just a minute to rid herself of a strange sorrow. Grief would have been personal; this was not grief, she told herself. It might have been sorrow at the passing of a human being, or maybe just a sense of futility after all of her and the doctor's hard work.

April decided not to wake the marshal. Quietly she

wrapped her shawl around her shoulders and went to find the doctor.

The doctor was easily awakened, and he walked with April back to the jail. They let themselves in quietly, and the doctor reached through the bars as April had done to try to find a pulse. There was none. He put his stethoscope on Bump's chest and listened for a long time. At length he went to April and patted her shoulder. There were many words that might have been said—about how hard they had worked, or how about Bump was a bad man who'd brought this on himself—but they remained silent. The doctor wrapped April's shawl around her shoulders and walked her back to the boardinghouse.

After seeing April safely home, the doctor returned to the marshal's office to see if Brink was awake. It was almost 2:00 A.M. There was a light on, so the doctor opened the door and stepped in to find the marshal asleep in his chair.

The marshal opened one eye. "It's all right, Doc, I'm awake. What do you need?"

"I just wanted to tell you that Bump died."

Brink sat up and rubbed his eyes. "Just now?" He looked into the cell.

"About twenty minutes ago."

Brink got up and opened the cell. He laid a blanket over Bump, covering his face. "So now it's a murder," he said grimly.

Some miles east of the border that separated the Territory of Wyoming from the State of Nebraska, in a low spot on the tracks, Nate Jackson was busy prying up rails and dragging them away with his team of mules. It was hard work for a banker, and he cursed Bump Hollister for getting himself arrested. He had had no idea that a single rail weighed so much. To get a rope around one, he had to lift one end with a pry bar and then slide a large rock under it to hold it up. His first few attempts had ended when the rope slid off the end. Finally he found a way to keep the rope from slipping, but then the end would dig in, and the mules would balk. He removed his coat and rolled up his sleeves, determined to accomplish the task.

Even though Stan Hollister was on foot, he had followed Nate out of town, managing to keep him in sight or hearing until Nate arrived at the grove where he had left the mule team. After Nate drove the wagon from the grove, Stan lay down for a few hours of sleep. When he awoke, it was a simple matter to follow the wagon tracks by starlight. From years of working in leg chains, Stan Hollister had the stamina of a mustang and the strength of a draft horse. He alternated running and walking along the trail left by Nate's wagon, and, when he lost the trail, he went to the railroad tracks until he could find the wagon tracks again. He had one goal: find Nate Jackson and kill him. And, after killing him, he would take Nate's role in what was clearly to be a train robbery.

Nate didn't want to merely stop the train. He wanted to leave it stranded for days, if possible. He would flag the train down to slow it as it ascended the grade out of the hollow, and the engineer would then see the missing rails and bring the train to a stop. The crew would have no choice but to stop the train, because, according to his plan, Ed Hollister and Abe would have them at gunpoint. Then he would have to do Bump's job, riding fast past the train to light a fuse to a charge of black powder that would blow up the tracks behind the train, trapping it. The cottonwoods along the creek bottom would hide the explosion from hearing and view in case there was a passing wagon train or Army patrol somewhere nearby on the prairie.

Nate had devised a scheme to keep the rails from digging into the soil. The next trick was to get the mules to back the wagon, dragging the rails to higher ground. He was forced to get out and stand between their heads, pushing back on their collars. He wouldn't be able to remove as many rails as he wanted to, but he could still make the track impassable. That was the main thing. He cursed the Hollisters frequently. With Bump's assistance, this job would have been easy.

If his brother and Ed Hollister did their part, when the train arrived, the passengers would be disarmed and locked in the cars, and the three men could find the safe and remove it. If they could open it where they found it, they would, and then they'd ride away in different directions. If not, with the train trapped, they'd still have plenty of time to haul the safe away in the wagon and open it later. The part of the plan that was not written down, that Nate had devised that very night, was that as soon as Ed Hollister turned his back, Nate would kill him. This had to be done soon; it wouldn't take Ed long to deduce that Nate had killed his brother, Bump.

Chapter Twenty-two

Jimmy and Penny found the conductor and told him that a passenger was missing.

"What do you mean, 'missing'?" he asked.

Penny answered, "He was here an hour ago, and now I can't find him. Anywhere."

"How well did you know this man?" The conductor looked with disapproving suspicion at Penny, a middle-aged woman wearing man's clothes.

"He's my husband!" Penny said.

"Would he have any reason to get off the train?"

"No. He had a ticket to Cheyenne," Penny answered. Jimmy looked at her and raised his eyebrows slightly. He remembered clearly that Abe had told him he was going on through, possibly to California. He started to ask her about her statement but changed his mind. He sensed that the conductor was not sympathetic to her problem, and he didn't want to muddy the waters.

The conductor sighed, letting them know that this situation was a burden for him. He said, "I'll look through the Pullman cars. You folks check the regular cars once more. Let me know as soon as you find him, so I can avoid disturbing any more passengers than necessary." By his tone he implied that it was their fault that someone was missing and that he probably wasn't missing, anyway.

Jimmy knew that it would be fruitless to search the passenger cars again, but unless they agreed to do so, he was afraid the conductor might not be diligent in his search. Jimmy and Penny methodically looked through all the passenger cars again without finding Abe. She told him Abe had walked to the back of the train, Ed Hollister had followed him, and then Ed came back alone. She was convinced that Ed had done something to Abe and that he was lying along the track some miles back.

"Do Abe and Ed know each other?" Jimmy asked.

"Yes," she replied, truthfully.

"Were they traveling together?"

"No," she lied. She realized how strange that sounded, but she couldn't think of a way to smooth it over.

"Where is this man, Ed Hollister, now?"

"I don't know," she answered, "but he was here after Abe disappeared."

"What does he look like, this Ed fellow?"

Penny described him. Jimmy thought he remembered

seeing the man but had not spoken to him or seen him talking with Abe or anyone else.

"Was he armed?"

"I think so. A rifle. Maybe a pistol too."

This was a peculiar situation for which Jimmy could find no logical explanation. Here were three people who knew one another, two of them man and wife, all traveling separately on one train to who knows where. He had instantly liked Abe and had talked with him at length on a variety of subjects. He couldn't help but empathize with Penny, who he believed was sincere, but this situation made no sense that he could see.

Ed Hollister was now wearing a heavy coat and knit cap for working on top of the train, and he had moved to a different seat. He saw two people walking down the aisle toward him and pulled his hat over his face. He wrapped a hand around the rifle that was leaning on the seat next to him.

As she passed by, Penny thought she recognized Ed but wasn't sure enough to wake a passenger who seemed to be sleeping. She hesitated, looked at Jimmy, and then looked both ways up and down the aisle. Ed Hollister was nowhere else in the car. This man must be he. She nudged Jimmy's elbow to alert him.

"Ed Hollister?" she said in a low voice.

Ed straightened up and looked at her. He hadn't recognized her either.

"Who wants to know?"

"Where's Abe? Penny asked. "Where's Abe Jackson?"

"How would I know?" he growled. "And what business is it of yours?"

Penny pulled her hat from her head. There was little light in the car, but she could see the flash of recognition on Ed's face.

"What happened? Where is he?" she repeated.

"I'm tending to my own business. Go tend to yours, and leave me alone."

There was an implied threat in his voice. Jimmy was sure the man was hiding something. He didn't like him, and he thought he was dangerous. He put his right hand on his gun and stepped in front of Penny.

"When you speak to this woman, speak politely, mister." Jimmy's heart was racing. He sensed that he was in a dangerous situation, but he was sure he was taking the right action. This woman needed help, and this man was thwarting her.

Ed decided that if this well-dressed young man was a railroad detective, there was no sense in antagonizing him. He could settle with him later.

"Sorry. I've been asleep. I haven't seen Abe for at least an hour."

Penny knew he was lying, and she again fought the urge to pull her derringer out of her pants pocket and shoot him—an act that would not help her find Abe, she acknowledged. She also sensed that Jimmy Whipwell was on the edge. One of the skills she had acquired from many years of dealing with men in saloons was anticipating trouble and avoiding it.

"Let's go." She pulled at Jimmy's sleeve.

Jimmy kept his eyes on Ed Hollister as he followed her down the aisle. Ed slumped in his seat and pulled his cap over his eyes. They reached the end of the train and walked forward again to meet the conductor.

"Did you find your friend?" he asked when they met.

"No," Jimmy replied.

"Hmm. I was sure you would," the conductor said, shaking his head. "There's no sign of him in the Pullman cars," he told them. He looked at them carefully to see if they understood the implications of the situation. "The only other explanation is that he fell from the train." He shook his head slowly. "If he's been missing for an hour, he could be twenty, twenty-five miles back."

"We have to find him," Penny said desperately.

He sighed, still shaking his head. "I'll leave a message at Ogallala for the eastbound train to watch for him. That's all I can do."

"How far are we from Ogallala?" Penny asked.

"Just a few miles now. The train will begin slowing soon."

Penny stood as straight as she could. "I'm going to get off at Ogallala and go back along the track."

The conductor shook his head in disapproval. "You can't start walking the track in the middle of the night. And twenty-five miles? You'd best wait for the eastbound to take you back."

"No. I can't wait. I know how to ride; I'll try to find a horse."

The conductor stated the obvious. "It's dark, ma'am. There are Indians around. There are wild animals." He leaned down to look directly into her eyes. "Your life will be in danger!"

"I'm going back," Penny insisted.

"I'm sure there are no horses available in Ogallala in the middle of the night."

Jimmy had been thinking. "Can you ride bareback, Penny?"

"I did as a girl."

Jimmy's horses were his future; they were all well-bred and valuable, but he couldn't let this woman walk away into the night alone. "I have horses on the train but only one saddle. "We'll unload my horses and ride back together."

It was a difficult decision for Jimmy. His newfound friend, Mary Ann Bringham, might not understand, and he would not even be able to explain it to her, since she was asleep. His potential job as a deputy in Cheyenne would probably be lost to him also, since Mary Ann was his future employer's daughter. He had to admit to himself that if he went ahead with this, he might never see Mary Ann again, or Cheyenne. But he remembered his father's admonition to do honor to the Whipwell name, and he was convinced that riding back to look for Abe Jackson was the right thing to do. Penny looked at him, and her expression softened. Men didn't usually treat her like this, not even Abe.

She put a hand on his chest. "Thank you. I can't repay you."

"We'll find your husband," he assured her, though he was afraid what they would find would be a body.

At Ogallala the train was delayed while Jimmy, by the light of a lamp, separated his stallion and the gelding from the other horses in the stock car and started to unload them.

Penny stopped him. She had come to a decision. "I don't want you to go with me," she said. "Just lend me a horse. I'll see that you get it back. I can pay you eighteen dollars for the use of it." It was all the money Penny had.

"I can't let you ride back alone," Jimmy protested.

"You're sweet on that girl from New York, aren't you?"

Jimmy hesitated, then nodded. "Yeah, I guess I am," he said.

Penny knew few of the details of the plan to rob the train and would not have revealed them if she had, but she didn't want innocent people to get hurt. "You have to stay on the train to protect her."

Jimmy's brow furrowed. This new information just added to the questions he already had.

"Don't ask me how I know, but this train is headed for trouble."

Jimmy leaned forward, his eyes wide, questioning. "Penny, you have to tell me what you know."

She shook her head. "Stay on the train," Penny repeated. "And be ready for trouble before you get to Pine Bluffs," she added.

"That's only a few miles west of here," he said.

"I know. You have to stay on the train. I have to go."

"You'll be in danger if you ride of alone."

"I'll be all right. Now please let me ride your easiest horse, and then get back on the train. Here's my eighteen dollars." She fished the money out of her shirt pocket, but Jimmy wouldn't take it.

"You keep it." He went to his gelding and put a halter on

him. He led him off the train, and a brakeman closed the door of the stock car.

The conductor approached them. He was not totally without sympathy, but he knew what his responsibility was. "Folks, I've lost too much time. This train is going to leave in two minutes."

Jimmy nodded at the conductor and handed the halter of the gelding to Penny, saying, "He's as good a horse for you as there is."

"I'll make sure you get him back, Jimmy, I promise. Thank you. Thank you very much." She took his hand for a moment and then dropped it, turning away.

The whistle blew, and the conductor called, "All aboard!"

Jimmy stroked his favorite gelding one last time, wished Penny good luck, and jumped back onto the train as it started to roll. He waited on the step as the train gathered speed, and he watched as Penny struggled up onto the back of the big gelding and then rode slowly across the platform and down the track to the east.

Ed Hollister was feeling good. He had found the plan for robbing the train that Abe had been hiding from him, and Abe was now lying on the track somewhere west of Sutherland. After pushing him from the platform of the speeding train, Ed had gone to Abe's seat, searched his coat, and found the notes that Nate had written for his brother. He would have preferred to shoot him, but he hadn't wanted the passengers to hear a shot. Falling from the platform of the speeding train would almost surely have killed him, and, even if it didn't, he wouldn't be in a position to do anything that might hinder Ed's revised plan.

Then Hollister had an idea. According to Nate's plan that he had taken from Abe's jacket, Nate would cut the telegraph line going east from Cheyenne. There was no reason not to cut the line that he could see from the train also. Then the train would be truly isolated.

The train seemed to be taking a long time at this stop. He thought it was Ogallala; perhaps they were loading passengers or freight here. He tried to see ahead to determine what the delay might be, but in the darkness he could see nothing. Then he saw a brakeman walk by with a lantern. At last, something was about to happen, he thought, and he was right. A few minutes later the train started rolling out of the station.

When the train was up to speed, and the brakemen were settled in one of the passenger cars, he carried his bag of tools and equipment to the roof of the last car. He tied the axe to one end of a long rope and tied the other end to a fixture on the top of the car. Then he whirled the axe around and let it go in the direction of the telegraph line. The axe flew through the night, and the rope wrapped around the wire as the train sped down the track. It not only caught the wire, but Hollister heard a crack as a crosstree snapped. He cut the rope when he heard the crosstree bounce along the track, following the train. Perfect, he thought. He shouldered his bag, descended the ladder to the platform, and made his way back to his seat.

Chapter Twenty-three

The marshal got a few more minutes of sleep before the telegrapher, Paul, woke him again.

"What is it, Paul?" His voice was thick with sleep.

"The telegraph line is down west of Ogallala," Paul said, and he watched the marshal's face to make sure he understood that this was a new break.

"What happened?"

"I don't know. North Platte could reach Sidney after the line went down west of here earlier. They wired me minutes ago, through Denver, that as of 3:00 A.M. they could no longer reach Sidney." He waited while the marshal digested this. "I wasn't very worried before, but something is wrong. I don't like this," he added, shaking his head.

The Marshal looked at his watch: 3:30 A.M. He wished he could get just a few more hours of sleep, but his daughter was on the train that was somewhere between the two breaks in the telegraph line.

"Do me a favor, Paul."

"Anything you want, Marshal, as long as I can get back to the office soon. Just in case something else—"

The marshal cut him off. "Sure. Go wake up Bob and tell him I want him to take over. I'm going to ride out to meet the train."

Paul whistled low. The situation was serious enough to warrant such an action. "You got it."

"Oh, and tell him the prisoner died." The marshal indicated the covered body of Bump, still in the cell.

Paul walked to the cell with his hat in hand, stood for a moment, and then left the office quickly to do the marshal's bidding.

Marshal Bringham pulled his boots on and slipped his arms through his vest. He took a rifle and a box of cartridges from his cabinet and grabbed a canteen. Then he donned his jacket and left his office, headed for the livery stable.

At the livery he saddled his own horse and then got a halter and put it on another horse that belonged to the stable. His intention was to alternate riding the two animals. He left a note for the owner of the livery that he had taken his horse. Then he mounted up and set out along the track going east. The sky was still dark; it was 3:45 A.M.

As he rode through the night, Brink thought about the events of the past week. The killing of his prisoner, the murderer who came to town and hired a wagon and then disappeared. These two events were possibly connected, but how?

The man who was killed had seemed like a good-natured drifter, but then Brink remembered how he had almost choked the bartender and how quickly he had pulled a gun during his jailbreak. He was a dangerous man who disguised it well under normal circumstances but was quick to react when offended. In Brink's experience, big men were usually more patient than other men because they could afford to be. This man had not been patient at all. It was hard to figure out a man after he was dead.

The man who'd hired the wagon had not seemed threatening either, just reticent and a little surly. Then the marshal had recognized him from a WANTED poster, but too late. The man had robbed a bank and killed a banker by beating him to death. Another vicious man concealing his nature beneath a placid demeanor. Had the guy with the wagon maybe followed the big guy to town just to kill him?

Once the big man was in jail, he had become an easy target for a murderer, especially one equipped with a shotgun. Brink made a mental note to devise some sort of opening in the outside wall of the cells that would prevent a similar incident in the future yet still allow ventilation.

I actually helped the murderer by putting the big guy in the cell. Brink swore under his breath at the thought. Then he had another thought. You would have to hate someone a heck of lot to seek revenge while he was in the custody of the authorities. But hatred as the sole motive didn't make sense. What if the man had been killed not out of revenge, but to silence him?

Silence him about what? What might Bump have possibly

said that would compel another to take his life? Brink thought about the man who'd rented a wagon and bought a considerable amount of tools, yet stayed in town until the big man was murdered, then disappeared.

They had a plan. They were going to do something together, and when the big guy got injured, his partner didn't want him anymore and was afraid of being betrayed by him.

That was an intriguing thought, and Brink examined it from end to end. If the premise were correct, what was their purpose in coming to Cheyenne? Were they merely passing through? No. If they were passing through, why did one of them hire a wagon days before the other was shot during his arrest? Why would a bank clerk turned bank robber partner up with a drifter?

Brink was too tired to deduce the pertinent facts. He was getting nowhere with his thinking, and he forced himself to consider something more pleasant—his daughter. She had wired him from Chicago, saying she had been delayed a day but would still be able to catch the Union Pacific in Omaha. And that meant that she was on the train he was going to meet. But was the train having some sort of problem?

In no time at all the marshal was thinking dark thoughts again, worried about his daughter and what might be happening on the train.

The sky ahead of him to the east was turning dark blue from black, and, at the horizon, the stars were fading. Brink urged his horse on, praising him out loud, startled at the sound of his own voice on the silent, dark prairie.

Chapter Twenty-four

East of Pine Bluffs, a perspiring Nate Jackson had removed four rails and dragged them a considerable distance away with his mule team. The sky was light, sunup was imminent, and he was satisfied with what he had done so far. Next, he took several cans of black powder down the track to the east about a quarter of a mile and dug a hole for them right under the end of a rail. He loosened the spikes on the rail for about twenty feet—not enough to derail the train as it passed over, he hoped. A derailed train would be much more difficult for three men to control. Passengers would disperse all around, and his accomplices on board could be injured. He just wanted the rails to be loose enough that the powder would lift the rail after the train passed to make it impossible for it to back up. The train must be trapped so that he and the others could get away. He did this to both sides of the track and laid a fuse out several feet. If the train was on time, it would be there within the hour. He picked up his tools and loaded them into the wagon and then pulled the wagon into the trees in the wash.

Stan Hollister could see the line of trees bordering the creek. He was still following Nate's wagon tracks, and they were headed straight for the grove of trees. As he approached, he carefully scanned the area, realizing that this was a likely spot for his brother's murderer to stop, if only to rest and water the animals. He wasn't sure precisely what the plan was, but knowing that his brother was on the train that would be passing here that morning, he believed something could happen in this creek bottom. When he heard the sound of Nate working on the rails, he crouched low and approached through the low brush that bordered the grove.

At Sidney, the train arrived an hour late, after sunrise, and the dispatcher told the conductor that the telegraph line was down in both directions. Because of the distance between the apparent breaks, he dismissed it as a coincidence. The eastbound train was still west of Rawlins, so that was not a concern.

The conductor agreed that there was probably nothing worrisome about the breaks, but he would have the brakemen climb a car occasionally to scan the prairie. He called, "All aboard!" The whistle blew, and the train began rolling on west.

Jimmy sat thoughtfully in his seat as the train left Sidney.

Penny had said something bad would happen before Pine Bluffs. He pulled his revolver from its holster and checked that it was loaded, although he already knew it was. It was a cap-and-ball Colt .44 that had been converted to cartridges. You had to remove the cylinder to load it, but it loaded in one-tenth of the time as a standard Colt .44. The weapon was well-cared for and worked like a fine watch. He replaced it in its holster. He wished he had been able to buy a spare cylinder for it; he wished he had a repeating rifle. But this weapon, in his hands, was as effective as any weapon could be, he was sure.

Jimmy turned around to look at the other passengers. He specifically looked for the man, Ed Hollister. He suspected, because of what Penny had told him, that Hollister was responsible for the disappearance of Abe Jackson. He also knew that Hollister was going to be part of the trouble that the train was heading for. He wanted to identify Hollister and be ready to take action to foil whatever trouble he was brewing.

Ed Hollister, feigning sleep, was also watching Jimmy, still convinced that he had some connection to law enforcement. Ed had had yet another idea. Without Abe to help him, it would be more difficult for him to take control of the train. The poorest passengers were riding in the passenger cars, which were last in line; there would be little profit in robbing them. Many of the men he had observed in those cars were wearing sidearms, which was another problem. The brakemen also rode in those cars between stations. If he could uncouple the last three cars after passing Bushnell, the last stop before the holdup site, he wouldn't have to worry about any of them. The problem was that he would have to do this in daylight. He set about making plans and in short order convinced himself that he could accomplish the task.

The marshal slowed his mount and stopped alongside Lodgepole Creek. He let both horses drink, then changed the saddle and bridle to the extra horse. He remounted and continued riding into the rising sun. He was exhausted but couldn't afford to rest. The horse, though strange to him, responded well to the reins, and soon they were loping along at the same rate as before, his own horse following on a tether. The morning sun had some heat in it, and it felt good on his face. He had been chilled when he stopped to change horses, but the activity, and now the sun, had restored him.

Mary Ann dressed and packed all her belongings in her suitcase, then walked down the aisle of her car to the passenger car to find Jimmy. She didn't know exactly where the train was, and when she found the conductor, she asked him.

"We've made up some time, ma'am. It will be about ten o'clock when we set to Cheyenne," he told her apologetically. He didn't like it when his train was late, and Mary Ann sensed his discontent.

"That will be fine," she reassured him. "This may be my last train trip for a while, and an extra hour won't bother me in the slightest."

He touched his hat brim and continued on his way. He had to make sure that the Pullman car was converted from sleeping accommodations to seating.

Mary Ann found Jimmy at the rear of his car. He had been walking from one of the string of passenger cars to the next, looking for something—he wasn't sure what. Most of the passengers were awake now, and none appeared to pose a threat.

"Good morning, Jimmy," Mary Ann greeted him in the aisle.

"Good morning, Mary Ann. Did you sleep well?"

"Oh, yes. I'm afraid I'm becoming accustomed to sleeping on the train, and I may not sleep as well in a bed that doesn't go anywhere." She laughed.

Jimmy smiled. This woman had completely captivated him, but he could not afford to relax and enjoy her company. He had to concentrate on the threat to her safety.

Mary Ann didn't want to embarrass Jimmy by asking him how he'd slept. She had sat on the thinly padded seats in the second-class car and couldn't understand how anyone could sleep on them.

"I did wake up once, I believe at Ogallala," Mary Ann said. "We were stopped there for quite a while, weren't we?"

"Yes," Jimmy replied. "There was some trouble on the train, and a passenger got off."

"My goodness, it seemed that we were stopped for a very long time just to let a passenger off." Mary Ann was curious about the trouble. Jimmy related the story of Abe's going missing and his wife's suddenly coming forward. As he told the story, he realized how bizarre it was. He was forced to admit that he had lent her a horse, and to do that, the train had had to position the stock car where the horse could get out safely.

"Will she return the horse to you?"

"I hope so. There was really nothing else to do. I offered to go with her, but she wouldn't hear of it."

Mary Ann thought the entire story absurd. Jimmy had been so proud of his horses, which appeared to her to be valuable animals. She didn't know whether to admire him for his generosity or condemn him for his foolishness. She changed the subject.

"Now that we're so close to the end of our journey, I see nothing wrong with your coming to my seat in the Pullman car. Would you like to?"

Jimmy glanced back down the row of seats in the passenger car. He didn't know what else he could do here, and as long as he was at her side, he could protect her. He replied, "That would be nice. Thank you." She turned with a flourish, and he followed her to the Pullman car. The train was pulling into Bushnell.

As the train pulled out of Bushnell, Ed Hollister got up, shouldered his bag, and walked toward the front of the train. On the way he passed two brakemen who, having assisted the train out of the station and onto the main track from the siding, were relaxing in a passenger car. They paid no attention to him.

He stopped on the platform between the passenger car and the Pullman. There was a curtain on the window in the door to the Pullman car, and it was still drawn. Good. Timing his moves to take advantage of the momentary slack between the cars on the uneven track, he lifted the coupling pin and uncoupled the last three passenger cars. He watched with satisfaction as they slowed and receded from the speeding locomotive, tender, stock car, freight car, and Pullman car, helplessly coasting to a stop. When the brakemen became aware of the slowing of the passenger cars, they rushed out onto the leading platform and shouted at Hollister over the hundred yards that separated them. He pulled his rifle out of his bag and levered a shell into the chamber. The brakemen retreated into the car, and within minutes the passenger cars were no longer in his sight.

Next he climbed on top of the Pullman car and crawled forward to make sure that the engineer didn't notice the absence of the rear cars. The tracks were so straight here that the men in the cab seldom had a view of the end of the train. From the stock car he could just make out the engineer and fireman in the cabin, operating the locomotive in a routine manner, unaware that they had left three cars behind on the Nebraska prairie.

Chapter Twenty-five

Stan Hollister watched Nate's preparations from behind a tree. It became apparent that Nate's efforts were intended to stop the westbound train, the train that his brother would be riding. He could see no reason to kill Nate before the hard work was done, and he found some entertainment in watching the man's bungling efforts with the mule team and the rails. He decided to let the scenario play out as long as possible before revealing himself.

Nate heard the train coming before he could see it. Rather than flag it down, he decided to park his wagon across the track, just beyond the missing rails. They might not stop for him, but they would stop when they saw the wagon and the missing rails. He waited at the bottom of the wash along the track and watched the train as it descended the hill.

The engineer saw the wagon and blew the whistle to signal the brakemen to apply the brakes, but the train kept going; there were no brakemen to screw down the brakes. The engineer could now see the disrupted rails ahead and reversed the engine with the Johnson bar. The backward-spinning wheels made a loud, screeching sound that could be heard over the steam whistle, now blowing continuously. Had the train been complete, it never would have stopped in time. As it was, the engineer had difficulty stopping the train short of the obviously dismantled track and nearly ran off the end of the last rail in place.

"Fred, get up on the tender and see why them brakemen ain't on the job!" he shouted.

Fred, the fireman, did as he was told and was about to report to the engineer that half the train was missing when he saw a man standing on the freight car with a rifle pointed in his direction.

"We got troubles, Brock," Fred said over his shoulder, not taking his eyes off the man and the rifle. The next thing he saw was a small explosion four hundred yards behind the train. They were now trapped.

After Nate detonated the powder charge, Ed approached the engineer and fireman across the top of the woodpile on the tender, keeping his rifle trained on them as he struggled with his footing. He threw two pieces of rope to the fireman. "Tie your friend up," he commanded. "Tight!" Then he added, "Start with his hands, then tie his feet."

Fred glared at him but complied with his instructions. When he was done, Ed had Fred tie his own feet together and then to a low fixture in the cab. Then Ed stepped down into the cab and tied the fireman's hands. Two gunshots sounded from the rear of the train.

"If you men try to get away, I'll shoot you. Just lie there and keep your mouths shut," Ed said. Then he climbed up onto the tender and ran back over the freight cars to the Pullman car.

When the train slowed, Jimmy knew that it should be pulling into the Pine Bluffs station, but something was wrong. The sound of the wheels was something he had never heard before. When the train stopped, it was on a slight up-hill grade, and he thought that likewise peculiar. He got up and looked out both sides of the car but could see nothing other than cottonwoods on either side. Then he heard a small explosion from down the track, and he went to the trailing door of the car. It was obvious something was very wrong; there were no more cars behind the Pullman car! Jimmy drew his gun and stepped out onto the platform.

By that time Nate had returned from setting the explosion and was tying his horse to the back of the train. When he saw Jimmy with a gun in his hand, he quickly drew his own weapon.

Jimmy was comfortable with guns, could shoot well, and had gone through training during his short service in the Civil War, but he had never shot another human being. Here he was in the situation he had envisioned for years; a bad man in his sights, with the chance to save innocent people, to prove his competence as an enforcer of the law. His finger hesitated on the trigger.

Nate took advantage of the hesitation by quickly getting off a shot, but he was not proficient with guns, and his shot went wild.

Jimmy reacted by jerking off a shot that also went wild. Jimmy jumped back into the car to get out of the line of fire. That's when someone came up behind him and hit him hard on the head with the barrel of a rifle.

Jimmy went down and didn't move. Mary Ann cried out in distress.

Ed Hollister whirled around quickly to keep his eye on the other passengers, most of whom were men. Some of them were carrying sidearms, but they seemed disinclined to use them. All raised their hands as Ed swung his rifle around to point at them.

"Get up here, Jackson!" he shouted to Nate.

Things were going well for the two train robbers who were left. The train was stopped and trapped. The crew was incapacitated. There was unlikely to be any interference from the well-to-do passengers, who would also provide more profit. But each man was missing his brother and therefore suspicious of the other. Nevertheless, they set about their tasks without delay.

Three miles to the west, Marshal Bringham heard the train whistle and then the screeching of its wheels. The sounds blended together to make a weird scream, the likes of which he had never heard before. He was trying to decipher the meaning of this unusual sound when it stopped, and seconds later he heard a dull thump. These were not the kinds of sounds that would reassure him. His horses were nearly spent, and he could not travel any faster. As he topped a rise, he paused, stood up in his stirrups, and thought he could see remnants of steam and smoke in the distance. There was a slight breeze blowing, and in seconds the horizon was clear. He shook his head and urged his horse forward.

Brink had found the first break in the telegraph line and had stopped long enough to see that there were fresh wagon tracks along the line. This reinforced his belief that the murderer on the WANTED poster, Nate Jackson, the man he could have arrested, had something to do with whatever difficulty the train might be facing. And whatever danger the train was in, that danger also threatened his daughter.

Marshal Bringham felt regret for not arresting Nate Jackson when he had the opportunity, for not taking the train east and meeting his daughter at some station and riding back with her through this mostly deserted prairie, for not leaving Cheyenne earlier that morning to stop whatever might be going on. But he had no time for second-guessing himself. He had to focus on the task ahead: get to the train, find his daughter, make her safe, then find Nate Jackson and arrest or kill him.

Nate climbed into the Pullman car, and, while Ed kept his rifle aimed at the passengers, Nate disarmed the men. He threw their guns as far out into the cottonwood grove as he could. He looked under their seats for rifles and shotguns but found none. When that was done, he walked back to Ed, stepping over the unconscious Jimmy Whipwell.

"Where's Abe?" he demanded gruffly.

Ed allowed a look of contempt to come over his face. "He stayed in Omaha with his floozy. Where's Bump?"

Nate shook his head in disgust. He didn't believe Ed. Abe would not have let him down, in spite of anything that Penny might say. "Bump got arrested in Cheyenne."

"Why didn't you break him out?"

"Yeah, that would have been smart. Then we'd have a posse running all over the country looking for us."

"What'd he do?" Ed asked.

"Shot at the marshal," he answered, "and missed," he added, as if that were the greater crime.

Ed took a few seconds to digest that news and then said, "All right. Let's get to work." He could always go back and break Bump out, or just wait until his brother served his time. He guessed that Nate would not want to surrender Bump's share of the money, but it didn't matter. He was going to kill Nate Jackson.

"Stay here and watch these yokels," Nate said. "I know where the money is. I'll get that, and then I'll come back, and we'll get what we can from these people."

"All right. Don't take too long." Ed briefly thought that Nate might try to take the bank shipment and ride away, but he could see both sides of the train and would have time to get several shots off with his rifle if he saw Nate ride off. He satisfied himself that Nate would be back.

After Nate left, Ed waved his rifle at the passengers, saying, "All you men throw your wallets and money belts into the aisle. You women throw your jewelry." The passengers hesitated, and he lifted the rifle to his shoulder. That was all the motivation they needed, and they began complying with his command. He added, "When my partner comes back, we're going to search you all. I'll kill anyone who's holding back anything." Two men then reached under their shirts to remove their money belts.

Mary Ann put a hand to her throat. She was wearing a pendant that her grandmother gave her before she left. It might not be valuable, but she wasn't about to let some common criminal have it. She put her arms at her sides, but she had given herself away.

The rifleman saw her touch her throat, and he made a mental note to find what she was attempting to hide.

Stan Hollister settled back and watched the activity at the train. It appeared to be going well, and he was content to let it unfold. His brother and Nate Jackson seemed to be cooperating, and there was little need for him to come out of hiding. He nonetheless kept his rifle ready. Then he heard a horse walking toward him from a few hundred yards back. He sank deeper into the grass.

Marshal Bringham topped the rise that overlooked the cottonwood hollow and saw the stopped train. He quickly dismounted, pulling his rifle from its scabbard, and led his horses to a tree. He tied them there, never taking his eyes off the train. He could see the wagon parked across the track, which explained why it was stopped. It looked like the same wagon that the stranger he now knew as Nate Jackson had rented in Cheyenne. If that were the case, a dangerous man was somewhere on that train or in the cottonwoods around it. *And Mary Ann is on that train.*

The cab of the engine appeared to be empty; Brink couldn't see the engineer or fireman. He saw a horse tied to the last car but no rider. The door to the mail car was open, and he assumed that someone was inside—maybe Nate Jackson or an accomplice. Bringham didn't want to do anything until he had determined how many outlaws there were and where Mary Ann was. Thinking about that, he realized there was only one passenger car on the train, a Pullman car. Mary Ann would be in that. This was the shortest train he had ever seen come to Cheyenne. Where was the rest of it? If the train had been broken apart by some means, maybe she was with those cars and, in that case, was in some other danger. Maybe she was perfectly safe somewhere on the track east of here. Bringham crept through the trees to a position where he could put the entire train within range of his rifle.

Stan Hollister was a mere fifty feet away, hidden from the marshal's view.

Chapter Twenty-six

Nate Jackson, in his years in the banking business, had seen several safes forced open and knew just where the weak spots were. This safe was relatively easy, and in ten minutes, working with tools he had brought, he forced the door open and removed the currency shipment he had known would be there. He jumped down and trotted to the cab to check on the fireman and engineer. After satisfying himself that there was no danger of their escaping their bonds any time soon, he hastened back to the Pullman car.

Nate entered the car behind Ed Hollister. "I got it," he said.

"Right," Ed answered. "Watch while I clean up the aisle."

Nate kept his shotgun ready, and Ed scooped up the passengers' belongings, which were lying in the aisle. He stowed them in the same bag in which he had carried his tools. When he came to Mary Ann, he grabbed her pendant and tore it from her neck. Then he exited the front of the car while Nate exited the rear.

Nate barred the rear door of the Pullman car and nailed the bar into place. He carried his bag of money, shotgun, and tools to the front, where Ed had already jumped to the ground and was trotting toward the stock car. Nate cursed. Ed was supposed to secure the front door, but he hadn't had time to tell him that detail of the plan. He had depended on Abe to do that.

When both men were out of the car, Mary Ann ran to Jimmy to see if he was alive. He was, and he was moving, but he did not respond to her voice. The loss of her grandmother's pendant and the serious injury to the man she had grown to like caused her to abandon her common sense and caution. She burst out of the car and chased Ed Hollister along the train. She had no plan; she was just refusing to give in.

Hollister was in the process of opening the stock-car door when she caught up with him.

The marshal sucked in his breath when he saw Mary Ann jump out of the Pullman car and run toward the front of the train. A robber was in front of her at the stock car, and Nate Jackson was behind her, bringing materials to block the front door of the car.

Marshal Bringham had seen enough. He recognized Nate Jackson, the murderer of at least two men and the greatest threat to his daughter in her young life. This was no time for formalities; he lined up his sights and squeezed off a shot from just over a hundred and fifty yards. Nate went down.

Hearing the shot, Ed whirled around with his rifle and fired several times, levering the action as fast as he could. He was competent with a rifle and managed to pin Marshal Bringham down with his volley. Then he grabbed Mary Ann with one hand and pushed the rifle barrel under her chin.

"Stop shooting, mister, or this girl dies!" Knowing nothing of their relationship, he had no idea of the impact that threat had on the lawman.

The air went out of Marshal Bringham. "Don't shoot!" he shouted. "I'll do what you say."

"Throw that rifle this direction," the bandit said. "Throw that six-gun too."

Stan decided he had watched enough. He stood up slowly and waved to his brother, then pointed his rifle at Marshal Bringham and said, "Do what he told you, mister. Now!"

Brink threw his revolver and his rifle out onto the grass in front of him. He stepped into the open but stayed back far enough that he could still duck behind the tree if one of them started to shoot at him. He had another revolver in his saddlebags, but his horse was several hundred yards away.

Ed shouted to his brother as he struggled to maintain control of a flashing Mary Ann. "Drag two horses out of that car, and find saddles and bridles. Hurry up!" At that moment Mary Ann pulled her wrist from his grasp, but before she could run, he hit her in the side by swinging his shotgun like a club.

She collapsed to the ground, unable to breathe for a moment. The pain in her side was almost too much for her. She lay on the ground, fighting to maintain consciousness. Finally she made her lungs work and gasped in air, her eyes wide.

Marshal Bringham nearly came out of his boots when he saw the rifleman hit Mary Ann, but there was nothing he could do while under his gun.

Stan walked to Ed, handed him his rifle, and then climbed into the stock car to find the horses. He saw Jimmy's beautiful mares, put bridles on two of them, and coaxed them to jump from the open car. He tied them to the door. Next, he climbed back into the car and found two saddles hanging on an inside wall. He took them down and placed them near the open door. Then he jumped to the ground and saddled both horses.

Ed tied Mary Ann's wrists together. She was still having trouble breathing, and every time she took a deep breath, she felt a pain in her side where he had struck her with the shotgun.

Stan led two horses to where Ed stood over Mary Ann. He poked the shotgun into Mary Ann's ribs, nearly causing her to faint from pain, and said, "Get up on that horse, lady."

Ed's eyebrows went up. "What do we want with her?" he asked. "What are you going to ride?"

"There's a horse tied to the last car," Stan replied as he kept his eye on Marshal Bringham, who had been taking small steps forward, trying to give himself a chance to intercede in some way. "And this little lady will keep our trail clear for a while." He looked at Mary Ann. "Get up on that horse, and do it now!"

Mary Ann mounted the mare, and Stan tied her hands to the saddle. Then he walked to where the marshal stood and tied his hands and feet, leaving him lying in the grass a hundred feet from the train.

Brink flexed the muscles in his wrists and ankles as the rope was tightened, hoping he would be able to get loose in time to give chase. There were more fresh horses in the stock car, and a saddle and a gun on his own horse, which was tied to a tree out of sight. These men were not going to escape him.

Stan returned to where the wounded Nate lay, leaning on one elbow. He spit in Nate's face. "Bump is dead, Ed." He looked at his brother as he spoke the words.

"I was kind of afraid of that. How'd he die?"

"This piece of dirt gunned him down in his cell with a shotgun." And with that said, Stan pulled a knife from his belt, leaned over, and cut Nate's throat without emotion.

Ed nodded his approval. "Let's get out of here," he said.

Stan went to the marshal where he lay, the knife still in his hands.

"If we're not followed, we'll set this lady free somewhere down the track toward Cheyenne. The eastbound will be along in a few hours; she can flag it down, and they'll come along and take care of you." He leaned down to make his final point. "So all you have to do is wait here, and nobody dies."

The marshal said nothing.

"If we're followed, I'll cut her throat and leave her for the birds. You'd better believe me." He gestured with his knife for emphasis.

"I believe you," the marshal answered, his face grim and taut.

"No," Stan said with a wicked smile. He was enjoying his power. "Say, 'I believe you'll cut her throat,' Marshal."

The Marshal had no choice. Every muscle in his body was tight, but he said the words, "I . . . believe you'll cut her throat."

Stan straightened up, smirked, and said, "Let's go." The two men and Mary Ann rode away without haste as Brink watched. They were riding single file with Mary Ann in the rear. Brink had never felt so helpless.

Chapter Twenty-seven

After the three riders went out of sight over the hill, several men began to work at forcing open the doors on the Pullman car. One of the ladies helped attend to Jimmy, who was regaining consciousness. The side of his face was covered with his blood, and she wiped it away as best she could. He tried several times to stand up and finally, with help, managed to do so. He had fallen on his gun, and therefore it was the only one that hadn't been thrown into the trees. One of the men picked it up and handed it to him. Another handed him his hat. Many of the men seemed to be looking to him for leadership. He had been the only man to draw his gun during the holdup.

A man with white hair said, "I hate to tell you this, but those outlaws took the young woman you were sitting with."

Jimmy's head was clearing. "You mean they rode off with her?"

"Yes. And I'm sorry for her."

Jimmy was nearly overcome by panic and despair. These outlaws were dangerous. In his mind, the abduction of a woman was as malevolent a crime as existed in human events.

"How long ago?" he asked grimly.

"About ten minutes. No more."

Jimmy removed the cylinder of his revolver and replaced the spent cartridge. A few minutes later the men were successful in opening the doors of the car, and Jimmy stepped down.

He pointed at the marshal where he lay, hands and feet bound. "Someone cut that man free." He looked at the lifeless form of Nate Jackson on the ground. "There's a tarpaulin in that wagon. You two"—he pointed at two passengers—"wrap this man up and put him into the wagon."

Though the youngest man in the group, Jimmy was having no trouble giving order. No one else seemed willing to take charge of the situation. Several men went to the marshal and began working on his bonds. The others walked out into the trees to look for their guns. Jimmy ran to the stock car and climbed in to find a horse. In minutes he had saddled it and let it jump to the ground. He was met by the marshal, who was now free.

The marshal quickly assessed Jimmy. He might have concluded, as others had, that Jimmy was a law enforcement officer, but Jimmy's voice didn't have quite that much authority. There was an air of immaturity about the young man that his clothes and sidearm couldn't disguise. But the dried blood on the side of his face hinted to the marshal that the young man would not back down from danger. In any case, he would need help to get Mary Ann back, and he looked fit and capable. The other men from the Pullman car were older, and the marshal doubted if many of them could even ride.

Jimmy looked at the marshal and saw his badge for the first time. He guessed that this was Marshal Bringham from Cheyenne, and he was embarrassed that he had been so ineffectual at preventing this crime. Further, he suddenly realized that if this was the marshal from Cheyenne, *it was his daughter who had been taken.*

"Who are you?" the Marshal asked bluntly.

"James Whipwell," Jimmy answered.

"I'm Marshal Bringham. I'm going after those train robbers, and I'll need help. I want you to come with me." The marshal's head was so full of concern for his daughter that Jimmy's name didn't register with him. It had been weeks since he had read Jimmy's letter. "We're in Nebraska, so I cant deputize you, but I have to have help." It was as much of a plea as a command.

Jimmy had been about to ask the same of the marshal before he knew who he was. He was going after the kidnappers and wanted the man's help.

"Hold my reins, Marshal. I have several horses in the stock car. I'll get a good one for you." Jimmy handed the reins to the marshal and climbed back into the stock car. He knew just which of his horses would serve the marshal best.

The marshal looked into the car as Jimmy selected a large

mare from what was left of his string. "Don't saddle her," the marshal said, "I've got a good saddle up on the hill."

"All right." Jimmy and the mare jumped out of the stock car, and he handed her reins to the marshal.

By this time the fireman and engineer had been freed, and the engineer was taking charge of his train once more. Like Jimmy, he had no trouble giving orders. He had several men bring the wagon up and directed them to find the rails and drag them back to the track. He inspected the damaged track behind the train, and his fireman, who had once worked on a railroad gang, began repairing the track where the charge of black powder had displaced the rails. The damage was fortunately light. The engineer intended to back down the track and find the rest of his train and then reverse and proceed into Cheyenne. It was important to him to accomplish this without having to be rescued by the Union Pacific. He was not about to steam into Cheyenne with part of his train missing.

After taking his saddle from his spent horse, Brink saddled Jimmy's big mare and then recovered his guns. Jimmy became impatient. Every minute that passed was like an hour to him, and he wanted to be riding hard over the prairie in pursuit of the outlaws and the young woman, just as he had read in stories of the West. He realized that they had stolen two of his good horses, and the animals' strength and endurance would make it difficult to catch them if they got too far away.

"If we're going to catch those men, we'd better get started," Jimmy urged. He didn't want the marshal to think that he was taking over, but his concern for Mary Ann overrode his self-interest.

The marshal grabbed Jimmy's reins just below his horse's chin and said, "We're not going to catch them."

"But . . ."

The marshal interrupted him. "Did you see how slowly they rode out? They're expecting us to follow them. They could be on the next rise with a rifle to discourage us."

"Yes, but—"

"And they might hurt Mary Ann." This was his real concern, of course.

"Your daughter. I'm sorry," Jimmy said, nodding sadly.

"You've met her, then?" The marshal watched Jimmy's face.

"Yes, sir. I have," Jimmy didn't elaborate. "What are we going to do?"

"We're going to meet them."

"Where?"

"Well, that'll be the trick. They said they were going to Cheyenne, but that doesn't make any sense at all. They won't go back to Ogallala, because we could use the telegraph line and railroad to chase them."

"They could abandon their horses and take the train east or west," Jimmy stated.

"Not likely. The engineer can identify them, and he'll have their description sent by telegraph to every train station from San Francisco to Chicago by tonight."

"They wouldn't go to Fort Laramie, because it's mostly wilderness and Indian country beyond there," Jimmy offered. Jimmy had studied maps of the West by the hour and was now familiar with the geography.

"I agree," the marshal replied.

Both men were silent. Jimmy, at first resenting the marshal, who had seemed somewhat slow of action and thought, now began to admire him for his thoughtful approach, as he, too, considered all the possibilities.

Jimmy helped the marshal hobble his tired horses so that they could be left in the cottonwood hollow where there was grass and water.

"Do you have a rifle?" the marshal asked.

"No," Jimmy replied.

"Let's see if there's one on the train somewhere."

The two men went to the engineer and asked him if he had a rifle they could borrow.

"Yes, sir, Marshal. It's not a repeater; it's a Remington .45–70 rolling block that I used to use to shoot buffalo. It loads fast." Then he added, "Haven't seen many buffalo lately." He looked out at the prairie beyond the cottonwoods. "I'll get it for you."

"How long before you get the track repaired?" Brink asked.

"We'll have the rail behind us repaired in an hour. There's four rails missing ahead of us; it'll take most of the day to get them back and spiked down. I'm gonna back up the train and find the other passenger cars, then I'll bring them up here. These here men aren't gonna be able to do much with those rails, but the passengers in the second-class cars aren't strangers to hard work." The engineer was referring to the fact that the Pullman passengers were well-to-do-middle-aged men and women, whereas the other passengers were mostly working class. "They'll get it done."

"That sounds like a plan. I don't think you'll see those outlaws anywhere along the line, but keep your eyes open."

"Yes, sir, I will. And they won't get a hold of my train again." The engineer climbed up into the cab and pulled out his rifle, which was wrapped in an old blanket. He handed it down to Jimmy. "You take this, and I'll go relieve one of those gents of his six-gun," he told Jimmy.

Jimmy took the gun. "How many cartridges do you have, sir?" he asked.

"I've got more than you'll want to carry on horseback." He picked up a box of cartridges, extracted ten of the huge rounds, and handed them to Jimmy.

"I see what you mean," Jimmy said, his eyes wide.

The marshal and Jimmy mounted their horses and rode out of the cottonwood grove.

The male passengers had found all four missing rails and were dragging the first of them back to the track behind the wagon. The engineer had one of them take a signal five hundred yards west, so that if the eastbound came along, they would know to slow down and watch the track carefully. In the meantime, the fireman had filled the hole the explosion had made behind the train and was spiking the rails back down. The track was missing one tie, but if they passed over that section slowly, it would hold.

The engineer enlisted one of the willing men to perform the

duties of fireman, so that his fireman could do the more dangerous brakemen's job. He explained to the others what they had to do to make the track passable and that he would return soon, after he had recovered his missing cars. He got up steam and was soon backing cautiously across the explosion repair. Then he advanced the throttle and disappeared out of the cottonwood hollow and out onto the prairie, backward.

The marshal asked Jimmy, "Can you read trail signs?"

"No," Jimmy replied.

"Very well. We'll do the best we can. It's been an hour since they left. We'll try to find their trail, and then we'll follow it for a ways. Maybe we can figure out where they're headed."

"All right," Jimmy said. In spite of the marshal's warning, he was still impatient. "Marshal?"

"Yeah?"

"I'm betting they're headed for Fort Morgan."

"Maybe," the marshal answered, "but there's not much left there since the Army pulled out."

Jimmy's eyebrows went up. "I didn't know the Army left. You mean there's nothing there?"

"I've heard there's a few settlers there and a stage station. Not much else. The Army even took down most of their buildings."

"The outlaws may not know that. I didn't."

"Well, it's a logical place for them to go. If the stage is still running, they can ride to Denver, and from there they would have a lot of options," the marshal theorized. "We'll see."

Chapter Twenty-eight

W hen Ed and Stan Hollister were well away and long out of hearing of the marshal, Stan asked, "We ain't really going to Cheyenne, are we?"

"No," Ed answered. "We're going to Fort Morgan. But we'll follow the train tracks for a mile or so. If they look, they'll think we're headed for Cheyenne."

About two miles down the railroad right-of-way the ground underfoot turned to smooth rock for many yards. Ed turned his horse around and stood up in the stirrups. He could see all the way back to the cottonwood grove where the train was stopped. There was no one in pursuit.

Ed turned his horse south and said to Stan, "This way."

Stan Hollister obeyed, and Mary Ann's horse, tied to Hollister's saddle, followed.

"Keep your horse on this rock, Stan. No tracks."

"Yeah, all right."

Ed occasionally looked back to see what kind of trail the horses might be leaving and was satisfied that there was nothing on the hard surface to indicate their passing. He also looked east to see if anyone was riding along the track, but he saw no one. When they reached the end of the rock, he picked up the pace, stretching the horses out. He kept to the low spots, out of sight of the railroad tracks, and Stan and Mary Ann followed. Now was the time to make some distance.

Mary Ann had conquered her initial fear and was thinking hard. Her hands were tied tightly to the saddle, but she managed to tear some lace off the sleeves of her dress and drop it when the men had their backs turned. She started with a big piece, wanting to ensure that her father would find it, and then she began to conserve the small amount of fabric that she could reach, dropping only small bits every few hundred yards.

The country was characterized by low, rolling hills covered with grass and occasional small conifers. They traveled between the low hills, wandering when they were forced to but always making their way south. From time to time Ed would ride to the top of a hill and look carefully in all directions, but he saw nothing of interest.

From the top of one hill, Ed checked the country behind them and then looked down at Stan and Mary Ann, weaving their way through the bottom. It had been a very good idea to have Stan come along. With Bump lying dead in a cell in Cheyenne, he would have had a tough task robbing the train and killing Nate Jackson. He had killed one Jackson brother, probably killed the other, and he and his brother had forty thousand dollars in cash and a nice collection of watches and rings. They had only to cross this prairie, and they would be free to enjoy their fortune somewhere in the West. Seeing no signs of life anywhere around them, he rode back down the hill and rejoined Stan.

"I'm startin' to think that marshal ain't gonna follow us," Stan said.

"He was the marshal from Cheyenne. We're in Nebraska. He's probably headed back to Cheyenne to notify the railroad."

But, having said this, Ed suddenly had a doubt. Why had the marshal been there in the first place? How had he happened to show up at the exact place where the train was stopped? Had Bump talked before he died? Was there something on the train that the marshal wanted? If so, Ed thought, the lawman would stay with the train, and that would be all right. He dismissed his concerns.

In the late afternoon they reached a little creek, and they dismounted and watered their horses.

"How far is it to Fort Morgan?" Stan asked his brother.

Ed had studied a map before leaving, because escape to Fort Morgan had been one of the possibilities. "From where we started, about seventy miles as the crow flies," he answered. From Fort Morgan, depending on the situation, they could go on to Denver on the stage, cross the Rockies to Salt Lake City, or provision up and head across the plains to Wichita. Denver and Wichita had reputations similar to

Omaha's—wide open and tolerant of fun-loving drifters, especially if they had money.

Stan asked another question. "How far have we come?"

"I guess about twenty-five miles."

"We've got a heck of a long way to go, then," Stan said sourly. In spite of his toughness, he wasn't adapting well to life on the prairie. The efforts required were more mental than physical.

"We're not going to stop in Fort Morgan. We can get water and food, but we have to keep moving."

Stan had other ideas. "I'm tired of this prairie. I'm gonna put that money to work in Fort Morgan."

Ed frowned. He knew he would have had the same argument with Bump, but Stan might be harder to persuade. He was less tolerant than Bump and hated taking orders from anyone, even his brother.

They couldn't afford to slow their flight. It seemed unlikely that they would be pursued, but once the train got to Cheyenne, the telegraph wires would be humming with news of the robbery. The most famous train robber in the West, Jesse James, always had a gang of men with him. He and his brother had done it with only minimum assistance from Nate Jackson, and their loot was probably one of the biggest hauls ever. There would be a reward, and there would be many men looking for them.

"We can't take the chance, Stan," Ed said. "We need to get as far from this railroad line as we can as fast as we can."

"You worry too much."

"And you've been in prison too long. There're telegraph lines all over this country now."

"If I ain't afraid of prison, I sure ain't afraid of a telegraph!"

"How about a dozen railroad detectives with shotguns?"

"If it comes to that, I'll deal with it, but I'm not gonna pass up a chance for some fun in Fort Morgan, or Denver, or Mexico City."

Ed knew that long years of imprisonment had left Stan with the feeling that there was no sense banking on the future or worrying about what tomorrow might bring. The important thing, to Stan's way of thinking, was not to let an opportunity for spending their newly acquired fortune go by. Ed was a little exasperated with his wayward brother. He needed to find a way to keep their escape on schedule.

"Tell you what, Stan," Ed said. "We'll get us some whiskey in Fort Morgan and then head on south to Denver or Santa Fe." Ed watched Stan's face to see how he accepted this. "We'll have a lot of fun all the way to Mexico, as long as we keep moving."

Holding more money than he had ever seen in his life, Stan had bigger ideas. "That don't sound like much fun to me. I think I'll spend a few days an' dollars in Fort Morgan," he said, grinning widely.

Ed gave up the argument with a scowl in his brother's direction. There was no sense in belaboring the point at this time. But he knew he wasn't man enough to face his brother down, should their relationship deteriorate.

"Get up on your horse, lady," Ed commanded.

Mary Ann did as she was told. She realized that the situation was completely out of her control. She thought perhaps that Ed was a little less dangerous than his brother—it might be better if Ed could make the decisions—but in the end it probably would make little difference.

"We can't make Fort Morgan before nightfall," Ed said. "We'll get as close as we can and find a place to camp for the night."

Stan got a cunning look on his face. "Let's split that money now, big brother."

By the tone of his brother's voice, Ed knew that this was a test, and that he would be wise not to fail it.

"Give me your saddlebags," he said tersely.

Stan handed his saddlebags to Ed, and Ed fisted money into them until about half the bills were in Stan's possession. He handed the bag back to Stan without comment.

Mary Ann was taking all this in. The contentious dialogue between the two brothers might be the precursor to a serious rife. She began to think about escape. If an argument became heated enough, she might be presented with an opportunity to ride away and hide. If she didn't escape, she was sure her future was not bright. They would eventually kill her.

Ed picked up the reins of Mary Ann's horse and turned his mount. The three of them pressed on southward, the late-afternoon sun on their right shoulders.

Chapter Twenty-nine

Marshal Bringham and Jimmy had gone almost two miles along the train track, following three sets of hoofprints that the marshal hoped were the right ones. Brink was beginning to get discouraged. This trail seemed to be heading for Cheyenne, and he was convinced that the outlaws were not that stupid. That would mean that they were wasting time following someone else's trail. The tracks looked recent enough; they were the freshest ones around, and they had been made by at least two different horses, maybe three. They continued following them. Brink had to be able to make an informed guess at their immediate destination so he could ride around them and be waiting there. He felt there was little chance of riding them down in this open country without endangering Mary Ann.

They came to a rocky surface along the track, and the

marshal lost the trail. He stopped and got off his horse to look closely at the rock. There was nothing unnatural to be seen. He looked west along the tracks and then south at the empty horizon. Fort Morgan was south. He continued to a spot along the tracks where the rock was again beneath a layer of sand. There were no tracks. He got down and walked along both sides of the track but saw nothing of interest. He mounted his horse and turned south, looking back to make sure Jimmy was following. Jimmy was completely without an idea; he had not even seen any of the tracks that the marshal had been following, but he fell in behind Bringham without protest.

In less than two hundred yards they were at the southern edge of the rock feature. The marshal dismounted again and walked slowly along the edge. There were no tracks at all here, and he knew that if the outlaws had turned south, their tracks would be obvious. As Bringham walked along, studying the ground, Jimmy rode slowly behind.

"Here!" the marshal exclaimed, and he put one knee on the ground. He pointed to the ground, and Jimmy got off his horse to get a better look.

In the sandy soil that bordered the flat rock Jimmy had no trouble seeing hoofprints. He walked along, following the tracks, until he found one made in the shade of a bush where the sand had been damp. The track was an almost perfect mold of a horseshoe.

"Marshal, do you see the pattern on this shoe?" he asked. Then he pointed at another. "And this one? And this one?"

"Yeah."

"Those are the shoes I put on all my horses. No one else has shoes like that."

The marshal let out a huge sigh. "Good. It sure looks like they're headed south." He added, "For Fort Morgan."

Something in the grass caught Jimmy's eye. He walked over and picked up a piece of lace. "This looks like the lace on the sleeve of the dress Mary Ann was wearing this morning," he said, turning the fabric over in his hands.

The marshal came and took it from him. This delicate fabric was on his daughter's person only hours before. He rubbed it between his fingers before stuffing it into his pocket.

"What do you think . . . about Mary Ann?" Jimmy asked quietly.

The marshal took a deep breath. "I have to tell myself that they'll want to keep her alive and unharmed until they get close to Fort Morgan. What they might do then, I won't speculate on."

"Can we get there first?"

"We have to. I know some roads that'll help. We're almost to Pine Bluffs, and there's a wagon road that goes straight south from there. That's where we'll start." They remounted and rode more rapidly than before toward Pine Bluffs.

At Pine Bluffs the marshal filled in the stationmaster on what had happened to the train. He wrote out a telegram explaining to his deputy that he was tracking Ed Hollister and one other man to Fort Morgan. The stationmaster promised to send it as soon as the line was repaired. Ed Hollister was now wanted for murder, train robbery, and kidnapping. Brink knew that Bob would alert the authorities at Greeley and Denver. Then he and Jimmy started down the road that led south from Pine Bluffs.

Each man kept his thoughts to himself, and, throughout the day they talked little. The marshal couldn't help noticing how strong and willing the big mare he rode was.

"Is this your horse, James?" he asked.

"Yes, sir. I had nine when I started out. I've lost a few along the way."

"What happened to them?"

"I lent one to a lady in Ogallala who had an emergency, and apparently the train robbers stole two more."

"What lady in Ogallala?"

"She and her husband were passengers, and he must have fallen off the train. I lent her a horse to go back and look for him."

"I hope it wasn't a very good horse," the marshal said.

"All my horses are good, Marshal," Jimmy said with just a small amount of regret. He had not had a chance to think about Penny and his gelding much, but he knew what the marshal meant and was forced to admit that he might never see the horse again.

The marshal said, "Well, this mare is certainly a good horse."

"Thanks, Marshal." Jimmy would ordinarily have launched into a discussion of how he had bred his horses, but his thoughts were too dark. "Marshal?"

"Yeah," Bringham replied as they rode along.

"This woman—Penny was her name—knew the man who shot at you from the train."

"Yeah?" The marshal thought for a moment. What sense did that make?

"Yes, sir. Her husband's name was Abe Jackson. I talked to him before he went missing. He seemed like a pretty decent sort."

"Jackson is the name of the man I shot. Nate Jackson."

Jimmy thought that over for a minute. "Penny warned me that the train was headed for trouble, but she wouldn't say what." Jimmy told the marshal what he knew about Penny: that she was disguised as a man, that she, Abe, and Ed Hollister had been traveling separately. That, upon hearing of the trouble, he, Jimmy had stayed with Mary Ann in the Pullman car. That when the trouble started, he had exchanged shots with one of the robbers but was hit from behind and knocked unconscious.

The marshal listened with interest but was too tired to think shrewdly enough to reach any conclusions.

Chapter Thirty

"All right, Stan. Let's stop here for the night."

It was a small creek with several cottonwood trees nearby. Ed stopped and got off his horse. The sun was nearly down, and both men felt there was little use in riding at night, as they couldn't be sure that they were traveling in the right direction. They were not riding on a road, although they sometimes followed wagon tracks. They had ridden to the Pawnee Buttes and passed them on the west side. Since passing them, Ed had been navigating by watching the peaks of the Rockies far to the west. His knowledge of the country was slight, but Stan had none at all. Ed knew that Fort Morgan was on the South Platte River, so they had only to ride until they came to its banks and then decide whether to follow the river upstream or down. He shared this information with Stan.

"We can't miss the river if we keep those mountains to our

right." He gestured at the peaks fading into darkness far to the west.

Stan was not completely reassured. "I ain't never been where the slate was so clean. I can't read this country. If you told me that we been ridin' in circles, I guess I'd believe it." His backside was sore from the saddle, and he was uneasy about not knowing where they were. Only the fact that his own brother was in charge kept him under control.

Ed tied Mary Ann's horse to a small tree and untied the knot that held her hands to the saddle. Then he hobbled his own horse and removed the saddle and bridle.

"Get off your horse, Missy," he told Mary Ann.

Mary Ann struggled out of her saddle and dropped awkwardly to the ground. Her hands were still tied together, and she had to release the saddle horn before her foot would reach the ground. Her legs were stiff from riding, her hands barely worked, and her wrists were raw from the rope. She paced around the prospective campsite to restore circulation to her legs and then squatted down with her legs folded under her and her dress spread out around her. She knew what her likely fate was, and she was desperate to think of some way out.

"Take care of her horse, Stan," Ed told his brother.

Stan gave Ed a dark look, shook his head, and then complied with his brother's command.

Ed turned to Mary Ann. "Missy, get off your butt and get a fire going.

"I can't do anything with my hands tied," she told him. She wasn't thinking of escape so much as just giving her wrists some relief.

"Oh, yeah, you can," Hollister said. "Get going!"

Mary Ann got to her feet and looked around. She hadn't been on a horse for this long in many years, and she was bone-weary. There were some dead bushes in the foliage along the creek and small branches that the wind had blown out of the few trees. With her hands tied she could only pick up a few sticks at a time. She would pick them up, carry them to where Ed indicated he wanted a fire, drop them next to him, then walk farther and farther on each trip to find more. Finally Hollister stopped her.

"That's enough, Missy. Get back here and make some smoke."

Ed had been looking at the low hillside that bordered the creek where the sun had turned the grass orange for a minute, then faded, leaving the grass a deep blue-green. They had been keeping a watchful eye behind them and had seen nothing and no one, but he wanted to make sure.

"Stan, I'm going to ride to the top of that ridge and see if I can spot anything."

Stan was pacing along the creek, working the stiffness out of his back and legs. He was grateful that Ed had volunteered for the short ride. But he was also the slightest bit uneasy as the darkness crept into the shallow bottom they had chosen for their camp. He could face the toughest guards, the most confining cell, the meanest fellow prisoners with no fear—actually, with relish. But this place had no guards, no bars, or even buildings, and twilight seemed to forebode peril.

"Keep an eye on that woman," Ed told Stan, and he started riding up the hill he had indicated.

Mary Ann was tending the fire, and as it caught and started burning freely, she sorted through the odds and ends of utensils and food Ed had been carrying. It wasn't lost on her that the two men were becoming a little cross with each other, or that Stan was not comfortable on this prairie. She hoped she could gain some advantage by exploiting this animosity.

"Your brother is taking a chance with this fire. If there's an Indian within ten miles, he'll see the smoke." She tried to make the comment seem casual, but she stole a look at his face.

"Shut up!" he said, but he immediately scanned the area around them.

At that moment a coyote howled, and Stan pulled his head down into his shoulders and looked left and right. Then he straightened up. "I reckon that's just a coyote," he said, wanting it to seem as if he was reassuring Mary Ann and not himself.

"Or a pack of wolves," she said slyly.

Stan levered a shell into his rifle.

Mary Ann looked, but there was no sharp knife in Ed's kit, so she began preparing what food he had. She would glance furtively at Stan from time to time, knowing that he was on edge. Stan was absorbed with watching the skyline. He had his rifle in his hand, nervously at the ready. Mary Ann felt that something dramatic was about to happen, and she wanted to be in a position to take advantage if at all possible.

An eagle had settled in for the night in a tree four hundred yards downstream, and it cried its evening cry.

"What was that?" Stan blurted.

"Wolf pack on a kill," Mary Ann replied matter-of-factly.

"Shut up!" Stan barked.

Two deer had been bedded down on the hillside opposite the hill that Ed was sitting on top of, scanning the prairie in the gathering darkness. They jumped to their feet and began running across the hill toward a gap. Stan brought his rifle up and fired off the cartridge that he had levered into it. Then, completely rattled, he levered the rest of the cartridges onto the ground without firing a shot.

Ed came galloping down the hill to see why Stan had fired. He reined up in front of his brother. "What happened?" he asked.

"Indians!" Stan said. "Three, maybe four. I think I got 'em!"

"With one shot?"

"Naw, I emptied the rifle. They were on the run, but I think I got 'em all."

"You only shot once, Stan," Ed snorted. "The rest of the cartridges are on the ground."

"That ain't true. Those are my empties. I got off five or six shots, at least." Stan had no idea how many cartridges had been in the repeater.

"We'll ask the little lady," Ed said, and he looked around for support from their prisoner.

But Mary Ann was gone.

As the sun set, the road became just two wagon ruts on the prairie. Jimmy was afraid they would lose the road and waste precious time, or, worse, deviate enough from their route to be seen or heard by the outlaws. Reluctantly he reined his horse to a stop.

"We'd better stop here for the night, Marshal," he said.

"I think we have enough starlight to ride," the marshal said quietly.

"Yeah, but it's important for us to keep going straight south. I'm afraid we'll lose our sense of direction and waste time, or get too close to Mary Ann and the two men."

One of the things that Bringham had worked at before being a marshal was sailing. He had worked his way up to second mate, sailing from New York to San Francisco.

"Do you know where the North Star is, Jimmy?"

"No, sir."

"Look here." He waited until Jimmy had turned his horse in the right direction. "See that star, right there, and then the one just above and the one just to the right?"

"Yeah, I think so," Jimmy said tentatively.

"Right there," the marshal repeated, and he extended his hand, pointing for emphasis. He wanted to make sure Jimmy saw the right star.

"Yeah, I see. I see it."

"Find the rest of the stars, seven in all, that look like a dipper with a bent handle. They're some of the brightest in that part of the sky."

"All right, I see them." Jimmy pointed at the stars to confirm. "There. And there."

"Now look at the two stars that make up the edge of the dipper farthest from the handle. They point right at the North Star." Brink pointed at each star and then swept his hand along their line until it pointed at the North Star.

"I'll be darned," Jimmy said.

"We'll just keep that star at our backs and ride slowly."

"That's a good trick. The North Star, eh?"

"Well, its actual name is Polaris."

"Polaris," Jimmy repeated. Only his mother would have had the patience to show him Polaris, but astronomy had been one of the few things about which she had no knowledge.

When Ed Hollister realized that Mary Ann had slipped away, he roared with fury. No words, just an animal bellow that resounded through the twilight. Then he turned to his brother in anger. "I told you to watch her, you idiot!"

Stan responded with a mighty blow to Ed's face that sent him reeling backward until he fell into the grass. Stan walked to where Ed lay, conscious but making no attempt to get to his feet. Stan and Ed had fought many times growing up, like most brothers. But this time could well be the last one. Ed had his hand on his belt gun, and Stan was ready to stomp on his brother's throat, but reason returned, to Ed first and then to Stan.

"All right," Ed said. "No matter." He kept his eyes on his brother. "She'll die out here anyway. Won't last long on foot."

Stan stepped back from his fallen brother. The deadly moment was over.

As if on cue, the sound of retreating hoofbeats came to the pair.

"She ain't on foot," Stan said. "I think she's got one of the horses!"

Ed stifled another epithet as he rolled onto one elbow and

got to his feet. He and Stan went to where the horses had been tied. One of the mares was missing, but its saddle was not. Ed gave the saddle a might kick in his disgust.

The girl had not dared take the time to saddle up; she had grabbed the horse's mane in her bound hands, jumped up onto her, and ridden her bareback into the night. She had little chance of escaping, but it must have been obvious to her that she had nothing to lose in trying.

Chapter Thirty-one

"**S**on, I believe I'm going to have to stop for a few hours," Marshal Bringham said in a low voice to Jimmy.

His feet felt as if they weighed fifty pounds each, and his lack of sleep made him feel as if he was walking uphill in sand. They had been walking their horses in the cool of the early-morning hours. With all he had been through in the last two days, the marshal had neglected to wind his watch, but Jimmy guessed it must be one or two hours after midnight.

"Marshal, I think there might be some water at the bottom of this hill. Let's keep going and see if I'm right."

"Very well. If there're some trees there, we could start a fire. Not much chance anyone would see it."

They had been following a long ridge that was laid out north and south, but now they detoured and made their way down the slope. At the bottom there was no water, just a dry creek bed. Without discussion they turned southward again along the dry creek. Jimmy turned his head from side to side to allow his eyes to better penetrate the darkness and finally saw a ragged shape that blanked out the stars.

"Marshal, there's some trees just ahead. There'll be water there."

"How far?"

"Can't tell." But the words were no more than out of his mouth when they nearly ran into a cottonwood.

"This'll have to do, James." The marshal tied his horse to a bush and leaned against the saddle. He had never been so tired.

"Sure, Marshal. I think I hear a trickle of water just down a ways; I'll fill your canteen for you." Jimmy tied his horse also.

"I've got a pot and some coffee, Brink said. "I'll get a fire going."

"No, Marshal, take a load off. Give me your pot and your canteen; when I get back, I'll make us a fire."

Ten minutes later there was a small fire burning and a potful of water sitting next to it. The horses were unsaddled and hobbled. The marshal had one blanket, which he wrapped around himself, but Jimmy had no bedroll. Both men were close to the fire, getting all the comfort they could from the flames.

"I haven't had a chance to ask you, James, but didn't I get a letter from you asking for a job?"

"Yes, sir." Jimmy tried to see the marshal's eyes, but they were closed—whether from the smoke or from weariness, he couldn't tell.

"Well, you seem to have a good head on your shoulders."

"Thanks, Marshal. I had a different idea of what our first meeting would be like."

"Yeah, me too," Brink replied. "I'm glad I've got your help. When we get . . . through this, we'll have some talking to do."

"Yes, sir." Jimmy paused, then asked, "When should we start out again?"

The marshal only had one cup. He took a drink of coffee, then handed it to Jimmy. "As soon as I get a little coffee into me, I'm gonna sleep a little," he said. "When the fire goes cold in an hour or so, we'll wake up."

"All right," Jimmy said, and he passed the cup back to the marshal and laid his head on his saddle.

Mary Ann had trouble staying on the mare as they climbed a hill, so she nudged her sideways to turn her along the sidehill. The mare obeyed, and Mary Ann made good time riding between the crest and the dry creek bottom. She crossed another dry creek where the ridge sloped down and then rode up another slope and continued her escape. In minutes she knew that she was no longer in view of the hillsides around the Hollisters' campsite. Holding herself on the mare's back with her bound hands and riding as hard as she could had put unbearable stress on her sore wrists, but it had accomplished something she hadn't been able to accomplish before—the rope had slipped down over the back of one hand. As she rode, she kept working the hand out until, finally, she was free! Then misfortune struck. Her efforts caused her to lose her grip on the mare's mane, and as the horse galloped along in the dark, she slipped and fell to the ground. The horse stopped running, but Mary Ann couldn't see her in the darkness and would not betray herself by calling out. She sat on the prairie and buried her face in her hands.

"Stan, you ever hit me again, you'd better finish the job," Ed Hollister told his brother.

"You shouldn't a' called me names," Stan replied.

Ed squarely faced his brother. "Never again, understand?"

"I ain't takin' any horse manure off of you, brother or not," Stan responded.

There was a long pause while each man sized up the other.

Finally Ed spoke. "All right. Let's get the fire going and get something to eat."

While Ed worked over the fire, Stan picked up the scattered cartridges and reloaded his rifle, glaring at his brother. They were silent as they ate the meal and then wrapped themselves in their blankets.

An hour after lying down, Jimmy was too cold to sleep. He woke up, shivering, and began saddling both horses by the light of a waning sliver of the moon that had just risen. He knew the sun would rise at about five, and, as there was no hint of light in the east, he decided it was not as late as four yet. When he had the horses saddled, he gently shook the marshal, and Brink was awake in an instant, in spite of his deep fatigue. He found the pot, which still had coffee in it, cold by now, took a drink, and stood up.

"Want some?" he asked Jimmy.

"No," Jimmy answered. The marshal poured the rest onto the ashes of the fire.

"All right, then, here's what we'll do." The marshal talked as he folded his blanket and tied it behind his saddle. "We'll ride until the sky begins to lighten, then we'll turn in the direction of the bright horizon."

"That'll put us in their path."

"Yeah, if we're ahead of them. And I think we are." They had mounted and were riding slowly, side by side, so that they could talk.

"Then what?" Jimmy asked.

"We'll have to watch carefully, so that if we come upon them, we see them before they see us. Just before sunrise, I want to be on the highest hill around. I have a spyglass in my saddlebags."

"Oh, good," Jimmy said. He was beginning to understand the plan.

"Yeah. We'll take turns scanning the prairie from the high ground."

"How far are we from Fort Morgan?" Jimmy asked.

"It's probably still nearly a day's ride."

"Startin' to wish I had brought a little something to eat," Jimmy complained.

"Jimmy," the marshal said, "I forgot. I think there're still a couple of biscuits in my saddlebags." He twisted around and reached into one, withdrawing a tin box. As the horses walked, he opened it and offered Jimmy the contents. There were four biscuits, and Jimmy took two. The marshal took the other two and replaced the tin in his saddlebag. They ate the biscuits as they rode, washing them down with water. They both felt as good as they could under the circumstances, and hope and anticipation quickened their pace.

The dark prairie was absolutely silent, and all its features were invisible. Mary Ann turned her head from side to side. She might as well have been blind and deaf. The only sensation was the cold that began to penetrate her clothing as she sat in the grass. She stood up slowly, afraid to make a sound, afraid that her captors were pursuing her silently and were ready to spring as soon as she revealed herself. She pushed a hand in front of her to make sure that at least the next two feet held no threats. As she took a slow, stealthy step, there was the slight rustle of her skirts, and her horse answered with a snort from a hundred feet away. She forced herself to think. She had been riding with a hillside on her left. She could feel the angle of the slope where she stood. If she continued walking with the upslope on her left, she would walk the ridge out and eventually find a wash or a creek. She might also get close enough to her horse to capture her.

Mary Ann walked for an hour and was finally too exhausted and dispirited to continue. Disoriented now, she was afraid she might be heading in the wrong direction. She had stayed warm while walking, but she knew it was going to be a long, cold night. She nearly fell down as she walked into a depression in the prairie. Standing still for a moment, she assessed the breeze and then lay down in the hollow and tried to sleep. The last thing she heard before drifting into a restless sleep was her horse, still apparently close by.

Marshal Bringham and Jimmy were still navigating by Polaris, but when the sky began to lighten in the east, they followed the marshal's plan and turned in that direction. When the marshal judged that there would soon be enough light to allow him to use his telescope, they found a hill that was at least a hundred feet higher than anything else around. They tied their horses below the crest and walked with their rifles and the telescope to the high spot. The view was commanding. There were ravines into which Brink couldn't see, but from experience he knew that those ravines were not easy to negotiate on horseback, and he assumed that anyone riding the country would ride the sidehills or even the ridges. He couldn't see the backslopes either, but he could see the country leading to and exiting from them.

The marshal extended the telescope, refocused the eyepiece, and began sweeping the prairie in a complete circle. He stopped frequently to watch various dark spots that he couldn't identify, and then, when it became apparent that the spot in his sights wasn't moving, he resumed sweeping. After making several sweeps, he handed the telescope to Jimmy.

Jimmy had never seen an instrument like it before. It took him a few minutes to get himself into a position where he could hold it steady. He would look through the eyepiece, then lower the telescope and look with his eye at the same scene. It was amazing to him, and he wanted to look up at the rising crescent moon, but he forced himself to attend to the job at hand. After sweeping several times, just as the marshal had, he handed the telescope back to Bringham.

Ed and Stan Hollister awakened. On the prairie the temperature often dropped several degrees just before the sun rose. Even though they had bedrolls, the sudden cold brought them awake, and, not trusting each other, each hastened to clear the cobweb of sleep.

There was nothing left of the fire. Ed began building another while Stan retrieved the two remaining horses, which had wandered down the creek a few hundred yards.

"Let the fire go," Stan growled. "We're gonna catch that woman."

"Not much chance of that now," Ed replied. "I'm going to have some coffee and some bacon." Ed cared little if Mary Ann was ever found.

Stan fumed, "I want that woman back. Let's get on the trail!"

"We're twenty-five miles from anywhere. We could run into a posse or a band of Indians at any time. You need me, so rein yourself in. I've got plenty of food; you can have the frying pan as soon as I'm done."

Stan's face turned red. What Ed had said made sense, but he was in no mood to compromise with his brother. "I ain't hungry."

"Stan, a city girl in a dress isn't going to get very far on a strange horse with no saddle," Ed reasoned. "We'll find her in the first mile." He lifted the pot from the fire he had just built; it was already hot. "Have some coffee and relax."

Stan kicked his cup into the creek. Ed stood up and faced his brother squarely. "Settle down. We've got a long day ahead of us." His tone was even and deliberate. He had used the tactic before to take the edge off Stan's fury.

"All right," Stan said as gruffly as he could. "Get done with the pan." He left to get more wood.

The rising sun temporarily masked most of the prairie directly east of the two riders, coating the image in the scope with a hazy blur.

"James, hold your hat so that it makes a shadow on the end of the telescope without blocking my view." Jimmy did as he was told. "Good. That helps a lot," the marshal told him. A few minutes later he handed the telescope to Jimmy, and as Jimmy swung the scope toward the sun, he shaded the front as Jimmy had done for him.

After taking several turns each, they stopped and rested their eyes. Neither voiced doubts about their tactics, but both were discouraged that they had seen nothing yet. The sun was well above the horizon. If the outlaws and Mary Ann were already south of their position, there would be no chance of catching them now.

Jimmy wondered what would have happened if they had chased directly after the outlaws. Would they have been able to catch them? Would they have been able to prevent the outlaws from hurting Mary Ann? As another hour of fruitless looking went by, he began to think they would have been better off chasing them as fast as they could.

The marshal, on the other hand, felt strongly that chasing them directly would have been much more dangerous to his daughter. But, he reluctantly admitted to himself, she was in so much danger either way that it might not have made any difference. He knew she could already be dead, but he pushed that thought away. He handed the telescope to Jimmy and said, "I need to walk around for a minute." He slid down the hill a short distance so that he would be out of sight of the prairie they had been searching. He stood up, groaning with the effort, and began pacing slowly, stopping now and then to stretch various muscles. He wouldn't consciously admit to himself what his intuition knew: that his reserves of energy were near rock-bottom, and he might not be able to carry on much longer. If it came to a moment when his daughter really needed him, he would have to be even more reliant on the young James Whipwell.

Chapter Thirty-two

Only a mile from her pursuers, Mary Ann forced herself to crawl out from under the bush where she had slept fitfully. In the gathering light of predawn she could make out details in the immediate environment and could even see the dim outline of her horse, still maintaining a little distance from her. She stood up and tried moving all her limbs. She was sore in every part of her body, cold, hungry, and scared, but at least her captors were nowhere in sight.

Mary Ann felt sure that her father would come for her, but the Hollisters would also be looking for her, and there were few hiding places on the prairie. She thought she might find a place where spring floods had created a steep wash and crouch there, but if she hid from her captors, how would her father find her? She could make her way back toward the railroad track, hoping to find her father, but that would take her toward the outlaws, and if she were recaptured, she knew she would be killed. In spite of her desperate situation, her independent spirit began to assert itself She resolved to rescue herself, and that would mean staying ahead of the outlaws.

The stylish boots Mary Ann was wearing had begun coming apart. She removed her petticoat and tore long strips from it, which she bound around her feet, boots and all. She stood up straight, smoothed her hair, brushed dirt from her clothing, took a deep breath, and began walking, keeping the brightening eastern sky at her left shoulder. Her horse followed her, but any attempt Mary Ann made to coax her closer was met with indifference.

Mary Ann skirted the tops of most of the hills, but every so often she gained a crest, and then she scanned the prairie in all directions. There was nothing to be seen except the sun hitting the peaks of the Rocky Mountains miles to the west. Satisfied that neither outlaws nor rescuers were in sight, she resumed walking.

The heat from the sun where it struck the left side of Mary Ann's face felt good, but it reminded her that by midday it would be very warm. She wanted a drink of water, a long drink, but there seemed to be no water anywhere on this prairie. Her makeshift shoes were holding up well, and as she walked, the stiffness went out of her legs. She lengthened her stride, hoping she could stay ahead of the lethal Hollister brothers.

"Let me have a look, now," Marshal Bringham said. He took the telescope from Jimmy and began scanning the prairie again. He was having trouble keeping his eyes open. The sun warmed his jacket, and he was getting too comfortable. He lowered the telescope for a minute and blinked. Then he took several deep breaths and put the glass to his eye again. The first thing he saw was an unsaddled horse walking slowly along a ridge about a mile away. He watched for a moment and then took the telescope from his eye. When he had the area identified in his mind's eye, he looked through the telescope once more and then handed it to Jimmy.

"There's a horse! There!" He pointed.

Jimmy held the scope to his eye and, after a brief search, found the horse. The telescope made the horse appear to be only a hundred yards away. He studied the horse for a minute.

"That's Jenny!" he exclaimed. "That's my three-year-old mare."

The marshal's first thought was that it must have been the horse that Mary Ann was riding, and she was either seriously hurt or dead. Then he realized that there were other possibilities, and he put his dark thoughts aside. He didn't have to tell Jimmy to scan the area around the horse; the boy was already doing it. The marshal strained to see what might be out there and found he could see the horse, but it was just a dark spot in the distant grass. What or who else was out there? Mary Ann? The Hollisters?

The horse went out of sight behind a low hill. Its path of travel would pass the hill where Jimmy and the marshal were, a half mile away.

"Bring our horses up, Marshal," Jimmy said, but Bringham was already walking down to the horses. The two men's thoughts were on the same track.

Jimmy tried to anticipate where the horse would reappear if it continued walking its apparent course. The low, rolling hills might let the mare stay out of sight if it began walking the bottoms. Jimmy stood up to gain the advantage of his height and tried to hold the telescope steady to his eye. At the point where he estimated the mare would reappear, he thought he saw a small figure emerge, but it was impossible to hold the telescope steady enough to be sure. He went down on one knee and tried again but saw nothing but grass. He lay down and steadied his elbows on the ground and focused on his point. He saw a head, then shoulders, then the entire body of a woman in a long dress, walking slowly. Mary Ann! The marshal returned with the horses.

"Marshal! I see Mary Ann!" The horse appeared, following Mary Ann about one hundred feet behind. "She's walking in front of the horse about forty paces."

The marshal took the telescope as Jimmy offered it and put it to his eye. He had no trouble holding it steady until he recognized his daughter. His heart sped up, and he began breathing faster, but it made no difference. His course of action was clear.

"Let's go," he said as he collapsed the telescope and put it into his pocket.

"Wait," Jimmy said suddenly. "Let me have the telescope again."

Bringham already had one foot in his stirrup. He swung up into the saddle and then handed the telescope back to Jimmy.

"I see something else," Jimmy said. Look there, on top of that ridge." He pointed to a spot about a half mile behind Mary Ann and looked up at the marshal to see if he could also see. Then he put the telescope to his eye and focused. "Yes," he affirmed, "it's the two men who took Mary Ann." He handed the scope back to the marshal, who collapsed it again.

"All right." Bringham spoke rapidly. "I'm going to ride to that hill there"—he pointed—"about five hundred yards in front of Mary Ann, and try to intercept her there."

Jimmy knew what the marshal was thinking. He said, "Right. I'll ride for the place she is right now. That'll put me between her and the men." He mounted without waiting for the marshal to agree. Once again the men were thinking alike, and each rode away on his respective mission—the marshal to be reunited with his daughter, Jimmy to put himself in harm's way and prevent the Hollisters from overtaking her.

The Hollisters had no idea that they were only a half mile behind Mary Ann and gaining, or that the authorities, in the persons of Marshal Bringham and Jimmy Whipwell, had spotted them and were closing in. They had eaten their morning meal in silence, each still angry with the other.

"What the heck's that?" Stan pointed at a horseman galloping their direction, just a little more than a half mile away.

Ed looked and said, "I don't know, but I doubt that he wants to help us." He had reined his horse in to get a better look. The horseman topped a ridge and then went downslope and out of sight briefly. Ed dismounted and brought his rifle to his shoulder.

When Jimmy came into view again, Ed and Stan began shooting, Ed with his .44-40 rifle and Stan with his Colt's Army .44. Jimmy heard the shots and saw the flashes. He pulled his horse up abruptly and jumped off while the horse was still moving. He lay down on the prairie, cocked his .45–70 and squeezed off a shot. He saw the dust puff about twenty feet in front of Ed Hollister.

Ed Hollister continued shooting, but his .44-40 did not have the range, and, worse, he was shooting offhand. Jimmy saw several puffs of dust in front of him and tried to ignore them as he looked at the rear sight of his single-shot rifle. He had not done much shooting with a rifle, and it was very disconcerting to be shot at, but he knew how to get a steady sight picture, and he knew how to pull a trigger. He made an adjustment to the rear sight and put another cartridge into the chamber as more puffs of dust rose on either side of him.

Ed had to elevate his barrel considerably for the bullets to travel the necessary distance. The sound was reaching Jimmy after the bullets raised dust. Stan, in the meantime, had emptied his revolver and was now performing the laborious task of reloading it.

Jimmy squeezed off another shot at Ed Hollister, considering him the bigger threat at the moment. The dust puff was closer to Hollister, right in line, but still short.

Ed had to stop to load his rifle. He was a veteran of the Civil War and had been shot at many times, but this was different; it was one on one, and the kid's shots were coming closer with each round. He nervously thumbed more cartridges into the magazine of the repeating rifle.

"When you get that short gun loaded, Stan, ride around behind him. I'll keep shooting from here."

Stan finished reloading and ran to catch his horse. He looked forward to getting in close; that was his kind of fighting. He wanted to be able to shoot from close range, or, better yet, go hand to hand with his fists and his knife.

Jimmy, outnumbered and as afraid as he had ever been in his life, stuck to his task in spite of his fears—just as his father would have. He made another adjustment to the rear sight of the .45–70 and inserted a cartridge.

Hollister, his rifle reloaded, began shooting again: work the lever, line up the sights, squeeze the trigger, work the lever, line up the sights, squeeze the trigger. As he began to make compensation for the distance, he also became more excited and thus gained nothing in accuracy. Work the lever, squeeze the trigger. Jimmy shot again, and this time the bullet hit Hollister in the boot heel. He yelled but kept shooting. He emptied his rifle again, shooting as fast as he could. Hollister's bullets were now kicking up dust behind and in front of Jimmy and to either side. As good a shot as Ed Hollister was, the distance and the fact that he was shooting rapid-fire from a standing position with nothing to rest the rifle on were too much to overcome. He was becoming frustrated and a little panicky.

Jimmy shot again, but Ed turned and grabbed his horse, vacating the spot where he had been standing, and the well-aimed bullet hit the ground harmlessly. Ed mounted and spurred his horse in the opposite direction. Jimmy had one more chance, but he heard a shot from behind him and turned to see Stan Hollister riding hard in his direction and shooting his revolver ineffectively from several hundred feet, closing fast.

Two more shots whistled by Jimmy before he could drop his rifle and draw his revolver. As Stan covered the last yards separating them, he stopped shooting, wanting to save two shots for close range. Jimmy likewise didn't shoot, unreasonably worried about shooting the mare he had recognized. Stan reined in the mare abruptly with one hand, revolver in the other, and tried to shoot, but the mare reared up on its hind legs and then turned its back, making it impossible for Stan to shoot at Jimmy.

Jimmy called to his mare, and as it wheeled around, it jumped forward at his command. Stan, no horseman, fell over the back of the saddle to the ground.

Jimmy ran to the fallen Hollister, revolver in hand. The fall had knocked the wind out of Stan, and as he struggled to his feet, Jimmy kicked the gun from his hand and then hit him hard in the side of the head with the barrel of his revolver.

Stan grabbed one of Jimmy's legs in one of his huge hands. It was like the bite of a grizzly bear. Jimmy smashed his revolver again into the side of Stan's head, nearly tearing his ear loose, but Stan hung on and groped with his other hand for any part of Jimmy he could get.

Jimmy, gun in hand, could have ended it with one shot, but this was different than shooting at someone over a distance. This man was right in front of him, and although he comprised a mortal threat, Jimmy tried to end it without killing. Again he smashed his revolver into Stan's head.

Stan's grip on Jimmy's leg relaxed, and he fell face forward, unconscious.

Ed Hollister watched the fight from a distance. He mounted up to ride to Stan's aid when he saw Stan fall from his horse, but when he saw Whipwell beat Stan to the ground, he pulled up. He already knew that Whipwell was deadly with a gun. If he rode in to kill the young man, Stan would be no help. On the other hand, if he resumed his escape to the south, Stan's conqueror would not be able to give chase. It was an easy choice for Ed Hollister.

Chapter Thirty-three

Mary Ann heard the sounds of the gunfight and turned around to see a distant figure riding hard away from her. While she was trying to fathom what that might mean, she heard another horse galloping, and she looked and saw a man riding directly toward her. She looked around—no place to hide, no where to run. She looked back at the man desperately. He looked familiar. She braced herself. But then . . . she recognized the man! It was her father! She felt light-headed, her legs wobbled, then she took two deep breaths and ran toward him.

Brink reined to a stop and jumped down, taking Mary Ann into his arms. While he was doing that, he never took his eyes off the prairie around him. He had heard the gunshots but had no idea what the outcome was. There were still two dangerous men nearby, and although he was joyful to have found his daughter, he knew that the danger was not past. He released her from his embrace and held her at arm's length. Her hair was matted, her face was dirty, her clothes were soiled, and her feet were wrapped in rags.

"Are you all right?" he asked.

"Yes, Dad," she whispered.

"You're safe now."

"I'm so tired." She put an arm around his neck and laid her head on his chest.

"I'm sure," he agreed. He looked around. Her horse was standing about a hundred feet away, watching curiously. He called to the horse, but the horse refused to come. He started to walk toward the animal, but it turned and made ready to run if he approached too closely. He gave up. He had no rope and wouldn't have known how to use it, anyway. He returned to Mary Ann and helped her onto his horse.

Once she was in the saddle, he patted her on the knee. "You're safe, Mary Ann."

She put her hand in his, and he squeezed it.

They began walking toward Fort Morgan, Brink leading the horse and looking in all directions around them, watching for the outlaws and for Jimmy Whipwell.

Stan Hollister lay near the top of one of the low, broad hills that characterized the prairie. Jimmy had tied Stan's hands tightly and then walked to the crest to see if he could see Ed Hollister anywhere. There was a light dust cloud to the south but no other sign. He returned to where Stan lay and picked up his revolver. It had one more shot in it. He poured some water onto Stan's bloody face. Seeing the torn flesh, he was shocked at his own brutality. He had to tell himself that he had had no other choice.

Stan began moaning, and Jimmy poured more water onto his face, then, remembering the strength of the man's grip, stepped back out of arm's reach.

"Get up, big man," Jimmy said loudly.

"Go to the devil!" Stan grunted.

Jimmy retrieved the buffalo rifle from where he had dropped it. He unloaded it and then held the barrel in both hands. He swung it like a club a few times, then walked back to Stan.

"Get up now!" he commanded, the stock of the rifle resting on his shoulder.

Stan glared, then awkwardly got his feet under him and slowly stood up.

Jimmy reloaded the buffalo rifle and mounted his stallion. "Get on your horse."

Stan looped his bound wrists over his saddle horn and pulled himself up onto the mare.

"I can't pick up the reins," Stan complained.

"You don't need them."

Jimmy grabbed the mare's reins and tied a loose knot in them so they wouldn't drag on the ground. He led off with the stallion, and the mare carrying Stan Hollister fell in behind. As they rode away, Jimmy turned around and looked at the mare.

"If he tries to ride away, dump him, Princess."

At the sound of her name, the mare whinnied, giving Stan

the impression that she had understood Jimmy's instructions.

Jimmy led the way over the crest and looked toward the spot where he thought he had last seen Mary Ann. He could see a horse and rider in the distance, but he couldn't recognize them. As he watched, the form separated, and he saw that it was a man leading a horse that was carrying a person, followed by a riderless horse. He rode in their direction.

Ed didn't even look over his shoulder as he galloped away. He cursed the fact that half the money was in the saddlebags that Stan had, but he had still realized more profit then he had expected to. He wasted little time wondering if his brother was alive or dead and whether he would ever see him again.

He told himself he could never return to Nebraska or Colorado again. He hoped he could find Fort Morgan and at the same time stay out of sight. From there he could catch the stage for Denver and then on to Santa Fe or California. Santa Fe might be just the place, but if his likeness started appearing there on WANTED posters, he could flee into California or Mexico.

Jimmy found the marshal and Mary Ann. His bashful mare was still following, but closer, as if she were slowly beginning to trust these people who were strangers to her. Mary Ann was riding the horse her father had been riding, another of Jimmy's mares, and the two horses recognized each other. When Jimmy rode up alongside them, he called to his mare, and she trotted obediently to him.

"Where's the other man?" the marshal asked.

"He hightailed it when the shooting started. I was too busy to see which way he went," Jimmy replied, stepping down from his mount.

"So I see," the marshal said, referring to the bloody Stan Hollister. Stan Hollister appeared to be a man who could always give a good accounting of himself, and James Whipwell, in spite of his clothes, appeared to be exactly what he was, a farm boy just reaching manhood. But Stan's head was gashed open, and Jimmy was virtually untouched.

"Looks like he got what he deserved," the marshal said.

"I guess," Jimmy replied.

"Keep an eye on him, son," the marshal said.

Brink searched Stan Hollister's pockets and found a leather wallet with some papers in it. One of the papers was a discharge from the Union Army. The marshal's eyebrows rose when he read the name.

"This man may be related to a fellow who was killed in my jail last week."

"My brother," Stan mumbled.

"How'd that happen?" Jimmy asked.

"Someone, probably Nate Jackson, poked a shotgun through the cell window and shot him with both barrels at close range."

Jimmy was feeling more and more like a peace officer. He said, "I hope we can apprehend the second man. He got away while I was dealing with this one."

The marshal remembered that Ed Hollister had made him say, *"I believe you'll cut her throat,"* and it made him clench his jaw.

"Yeah, I want him real bad too," he said grimly.

"I think it's best we stay together, now, Marshal," Jimmy said, and he rolled his eyes toward Mary Ann to tip the marshal to his meaning without alarming her. They were still very vulnerable on the open prairie, even though they outnumbered their sole remaining adversary, Ed Hollister.

"Yeah, you're right," Bringham agreed.

"Hollister, slide out of that saddle and get on that mare that doesn't have one," the marshal said.

When Stan hesitated, Jimmy picked up the big rifle. Stan wanted no more of that, so he complied, needing help to get up onto the barebacked mare. Jimmy fashioned a halter from another piece of rope so that he could lead the mare. Then the marshal mounted Hollister's horse, and they all resumed their ride toward Fort Morgan.

Chapter Thirty-four

Ed Hollister found the South Platte River in the middle of the afternoon. There was a road along the north side of the river, and he looked both ways on the road but could not determine in which direction he would find Fort Morgan, so he decided to travel westward. His reasoning was that if Fort Morgan were behind him to the east, he would just continue on to Denver. That would mean maybe two more nights on the road, but there would probably be lodging along the way. On the other hand, if he turned east and didn't find Fort Morgan, Julesburg was a long way away.

After traveling along the road for a while, he came to a likely-looking ford across the wide South Platte and managed to get to the south side. There was a road on this side, and presently he came to a crude sign that read, FORT MORGAN - 1 MILE. Ten minutes later he arrived at a scattered collection of

cabins, a deserted-looking stagecoach station, and the re-
mains of an Army post. He had expected more.

Ed rode up to the stage station, tied his horse to a rail, and
walked up to the door. He knocked and waited. Eventually
he heard footsteps, and a tiny door at eye level opened.

"What do you want?" a voice asked.

"When does the stage come through?" Ed asked.

The voice chuckled. "Your guess is as good as mine."

"Isn't this the stage station?" Ed asked.

"Yeah," the voice answered, and then the viewing door
closed.

Ed looked around, wondering if it was worth his time to
kick the door in, when the main door opened.

"Come on in, mister," the man inside said.

Ed walked in and looked around. This had been a modern
stagecoach station at one time, but it was in a state of disre-
pair now. There was a small bar at one side of the room, but
there were only two bottles on the shelf behind it and a large
cracked mirror on the wall. Ed could see an empty kitchen
through an open door. There were two tables but only two
chairs in the main room. There had been glass in the windows, but now they were open to the weather unless the shutters were swung shut.

The man who had let Ed in stood with his hands in his
back pockets. "The coach is in Denver right now," he explained. "It won't come this way until he has at least three
passengers."

"That's a heck of a way to run a business," Ed grumbled.

The man smiled and shrugged. "It's really not a business

anymore. The railroad has taken the business. Charlie just likes driving stagecoach, so he makes a trip when he can."

"And there's no coach going to Denver?"

"Not until he comes *from* Denver. There's just one."

"Can I stay here tonight?" Ed asked.

"Sure. Do you have any bedding?"

"Yeah."

"All right. My name is Henry. We'll give you supper and breakfast for two dollars and throw the room in for free."

"We?"

"My wife and I."

"Do you have someone to take care of my horse?"

Henry just smiled and shook his head.

"All right, then. I'm going to go take care of her."

"You can feed her from what's in the barn for two bits a day."

"Yeah, all right," Ed muttered.

"We'll feed you when you're done," Henry said.

Ed walked outside and looked over the rest of the town. He saw no one, although he thought that several of the cabins might have occupants at least some of the time. He led his horse into the corral and removed its saddle and bridle. In the barn he threw his saddle over a rail, then he found some oats and poured them onto a bench for the mare. There was water in a trough, so he picked up his saddlebags and bedroll and walked back to the house.

The marshal, Jimmy, and Mary Ann reached Fort Morgan when the sun was just over the mountains to the west. The marshal was near total exhaustion and was fighting sleep in his saddle, but Jimmy, although tired, had never given up watching for Ed Hollister as they crossed the prairie and then the river. Now in the lead, he reined his horse in and looked the settlement over carefully. The others stopped behind him.

"Marshal," Jimmy said softly.

The marshal heard Jimmy's tone and was instantly alert. "Yeah?"

"I recognize that horse in the corral."

"Is it one of yours?"

"No," Jimmy responded, "but I've seen it twice. The man who shot at me on the train was riding it, and I saw it again when Hollister and I had our shootout. The other man rode it away." Jimmy was surprised that he had remembered anything other than bullets coming too close for comfort in both instances. But he habitually evaluated every horse he saw, and that's what had helped him remember this horse, even while being shot at.

"That's the stagecoach station."

"He must be in there."

"He'll have to come out sooner or later," Bringham offered.

"I'm not going to take the chance of confronting him in the dark," Jimmy said.

"James, there's a man and his wife in there, maybe others," the marshal warned.

"He's seen me on the train, but the car was dark." Jimmy

was thinking out loud. "And he saw me at a distance today." He paused while he thought.

"That's taking a big chance," the marshal said.

Jimmy shook his head. "Marshal, if we trade jackets and hats, I don't think he'll recognize me."

"I'm going with you," Bringham said.

Jimmy looked at Mary Ann. She had been through so much, and now, the prospect of being left alone while her father went to confront an outlaw was almost too much for her. Jimmy could see it in her eyes, and he likewise knew that the marshal was too tired to be counted upon.

"No, you stay with your daughter. I can do this without firing a shot." He added grimly, "And if I do have to shoot, I won't miss this time."

The marshal looked at his daughter and immediately saw why Jimmy wanted to confront Ed Hollister without him. Her eyes were pleading with him not to leave her, and she was trembling. The evening was cool. The marshal patted her hand and turned back to Jimmy. "Don't let him shoot first, James. He's dangerous." The marshal removed his jacket and handed it over.

Jimmy nodded; those were his own thoughts. He removed his jacket and handed it to the marshal, who wrapped it around Mary Ann. Then, as he donned the marshal's jacket and hat in exchange, he looked into Mary Ann's eyes, wanting to reassure her that everything was going to be fine. He didn't know what to say, but Mary Ann clearly took comfort from his look.

He had reloaded his gun, but he pulled it from its holster and checked it.

"I'll be back in a few minutes." And he rode slowly toward the stage station while the marshal and Mary Ann watched.

Stan Hollister, knowing how good his brother was with a gun, sat and waited, sure that the outcome would be in his brother's favor.

Chapter Thirty-five

Ed set his saddlebags on the floor and sat down at the table. The shutters had been closed on the windows for protection against night-flying insects, and the room was dimly lit by a lamp on a shelf near the kitchen and a candle on Ed's table. He looked at the meal he had been served. It was ham, potatoes, and some kind of wild greens, and it looked at least edible, maybe even tasty. It made him realize how much he longed to be back in civilized society and to be done with this prairie wilderness. He picked up his fork, examined it next to the candle on the table, decided it was acceptably clean, and began eating.

"What would you like to drink?" It was the proprietor's wife, Barbara.

Ed looked at the woman. She was pleasant-looking but thin, a woman in her midforties. He glanced at the bar and concluded that there would be no whiskey, so he asked for water. Barbara went back to the kitchen.

The door opened, and he looked up to see a man of average height walk in. Ed studied him carefully, but the man slowly removed his hat with the hand closest to Ed, and his face was difficult to see clearly. It was not only that he looked familiar, it was that he seemed more alert than an ordinary traveler, perhaps even on edge. Ed casually reached into his saddlebag and put his hand around the handle of his revolver. The man gave him only a quick look and then turned away to survey the rest of the room.

Jimmy had seen Ed Hollister reach into his saddlebag and guessed what was inside. Ed had only gotten a brief look at him in the darkened passenger car. Was the change of coat and hat enough to make him seem a stranger? He looked around to see if he could find an excuse to get behind Hollister. He walked to the bar and put one foot up on the rail as nonchalantly as he could. He turned his back on Ed but tried to keep him in sight in the mirror without seeming obvious.

Ed thought about calling out to this suspicious stranger to get him to turn around, but he was distracted by Barbara's returning with a pitcher of water and a cup for him. As she was putting the pitcher and cup on the table, her husband came in to see what Jimmy wanted.

"Mister," he greeted Jimmy. "What can we do for you?"

Jimmy had had nothing but two biscuits to eat in the last two days. He had been too involved in the pursuit to realize it until now.

"Food" was all he said.

"Sure, son," Henry replied. "You staying the night?"

Jimmy didn't know how to answer. He hesitated until he realized that Ed was listening and was waiting for his reply.

"No, I don't believe so." He glanced quickly at Ed and said, "I think I'll go a few more miles before I quit for the night." He thought he could see Ed relax, but the man's hand was still resting on his saddlebag.

"Well, have a seat. It'll take just a minute to dish you up some supper," Henry said.

Henry looked at Ed and said, "By the way, gents, you can wash up if you want. There's a pitcher and basin just outside the back door. Through the kitchen."

Jimmy thought this was his chance. He left the bar as if he were going to walk toward the kitchen. His path would take him behind Hollister.

Ed still hadn't recognized the stranger, but he was too suspicious to let the man walk behind him. He had chosen this spot because the rest of the room would be in his sight, and he was not about to relinquish that advantage. He spun in his chair, pulling the pistol from his saddlebag as he did.

Jimmy saw the pistol and kicked out, knocking it out of Hollister's hand and across the room. Hollister grabbed his knife from the table with one hand and with the other hand grabbed a handful of Barbara's dress. As Jimmy drew his revolver, Hollister yanked Barbara in front of himself and put the knife to her throat.

"Put the gun down, mister," Hollister said.

"No," Jimmy replied, "you let that woman go."

"Put it down or I'll cut her throat," Ed vowed.

Jimmy could see the blade depressing the skin on the woman's neck. He expected to see blood spurt out at any moment.

"If you hurt that woman, I'll shoot off both your arms." Jimmy tried to sound confident and authoritarian. He somehow knew that the woman's best chance lay with him, though he wasn't sure just how.

Hollister began backing up toward the front door. His knife was now starting to draw blood as he struggled with the terrified woman. Jimmy followed and slowly raised his revolver.

While this was happening, the woman's husband, Henry, had picked up Ed's revolver from the floor where it had landed after Jimmy kicked it and now leveled it at Jimmy. "Do as the man asked you, mister," he said. "Put the gun down."

Jimmy and Hollister both looked at Henry in surprise.

"Stay out of it!" Jimmy said, and he again concentrated on Hollister.

Ed turned back to Jimmy. "This woman will die in three seconds if you don't drop your gun!"

Jimmy quickly evaluated his chances of shooting the outlaw without hurting the woman. There wasn't enough of the robber exposed to give him confidence, in spite of the woman's slight build and in spite of his own accuracy with a handgun.

Apparently Henry had seen enough. He shot at Jimmy from across the room. The bullet ripped across the back of the marshal's jacket and Jimmy's shirt and continued into the wall. Jimmy felt fire in both shoulders but held steady. Ed involuntarily turned toward the sound of the gunshot, and Jimmy quickly raised his revolver to eye level to use the sights. He squeezed the trigger and shot Hollister in the head. The outlaw dropped the knife and covered his face with both hands. Barbara stumbled forward, falling to the floor.

Jimmy quickly turned to cover Henry, but it wasn't necessary. Henry dropped the pistol and rushed to his wife where she lay. Jimmy lowered the hammer on his gun as he watched Henry gather Barbara into his arms.

The outlaw had dropped to his knees, still covering his face. Blood from his wound dripped from both elbows of his shirt. He rasped a curse and then fell forward, dead.

Henry looked up at Jimmy. "I'm sorry," he said. "I'm sorry," he repeated. "I'm sorry." And he hugged his wife tightly, rocking back and forth.

Jimmy looked at the lifeless form of Ed Hollister and then at the couple embracing on the floor. "Is she all right?" he asked.

Henry released his wife and held her at arm's length.

"I'm all right," she said to him.

He touched her neck where the knife had begun to draw blood.

"I'm all right," she repeated.

They got to their feet, and Henry came to where Jimmy stood, still in awe of all that had happened in under a minute.

"I'm sorry, mister. I was afraid he would kill Barbara."

"I know," Jimmy said, and he shrugged. "Is there a marshal here?"

"No. There's nobody here right now except my wife and me. They're all out taking their herds to summer range."

"All right. The Cheyenne marshal is outside. I guess he can handle this shooting."

Marshal Bringham heard both shots and told Mary Ann to sit tight. Two shots. That could mean anything, but his confidence in the young Whipwell had been growing since their first meeting. He was walking toward the building when Jimmy stepped out.

"It's over, Marshal," Jimmy said. He sat down on a bench in front of the stage station and leaned over with his elbows on his knees, staring at the ground.

The marshal turned and walked back to Mary Ann, still sitting on her horse. She was relieved to see that Jimmy was apparently unhurt and managed a weak smile for her father. He nodded to her and then led his horse and the one carrying Stan Hollister toward the station. She followed on her horse but dismounted at the front door of the station. Her father took the reins of her horse and put all the animals into the corral. He tied Stan's feet and then tied his hands to the corral fence.

Mary Ann went to Jimmy and saw the blood staining the marshal's jacket. He looked up as she approached with concern in her eyes. "Jimmy! Are you all right?" She leaned over to look at his face.

"Yeah, Mary Ann. I think I got a scratch." He tried to look over one shoulder.

Mary Ann lifted up the back of her father's jacket to better see. The back of Jimmy's shirt had a lot of blood on it. "That's more than a scratch, Jimmy. Come on, I need to take care of that."

Jimmy remembered the body of Ed Hollister just inside the door. "No, Mary Ann. Stay out here. Sit. I'll be right back."

The marshal came to the front door, and he and Jimmy entered the stage station. Once inside, Bringham inspected his jacket.

"I think I ruined your jacket, Marshal," Jimmy said with a wry grin.

"Mary Ann will fix it." Bringham took a small notebook and a pencil from one of the pockets. "Tell me what happened."

While Jimmy related the story, Henry came back into the room from the kitchen. Jimmy downplayed Henry's attempt to shoot him and instead described it as a deliberate attempt by Henry to distract Hollister by discharging the pistol, hitting Jimmy by mistake in the excitement. Jimmy left the marshal talking with Henry and rejoined Mary Ann on the porch.

The marshal stood over the body of Ed Hollister and saw the bullet hole just under one eye. He was remembering how Whipwell had bragged about his proficiency with firearms in his letter of inquiry about a job. Considering Ed Hollister's fate, it seemed much less like a brag now.

The marshal sat back down to make a few more notes and then looked at Henry. "Can you read?" he asked the man.

"Yes, sir," Henry answered.

The marshal handed the notebook to Henry. "Read this and see if you can think of anything else."

Henry read the notes, nodding in spots. "That's just the way it happened, Marshal," he said, handing the notebook back to Brink.

"Fine. I'll have my deputy read it too." The marshal realized with surprise what he had said, but it made no difference to this man, so he didn't bother correcting himself. He realized that he had been relying on Jimmy the same way he relied on his deputies, and it didn't seem wrong. He opened the door and asked Jimmy to come in.

Jimmy read the page of the notebook and without saying a word signed the page just as he had read in a detective magazine once. The marshal's eyebrows went up, but he said nothing as he accepted the notebook from Jimmy.

Jimmy opened Hollister's saddlebags and looked through them. He found the money, but rather than make a display of counting it, he just pushed it back in and slung the bag gingerly over his shoulder.

Jimmy and the marshal picked up the body of Ed Hollister and carried it out of the station to the barn. They were winded when they were done. It had been a long two days. The marshal opened the saddlebags of Stan Hollister's horse, which Mary Ann had been riding.

"It looks like we've recovered the money that was stolen from the train," he said.

"There's more," Jimmy said. "These are his brother's saddlebags, and they're full too." He pulled the flap open on one to show the wads of bills.

"Very good." The marshal tilted his head in appreciation. "You're probably in line for a reward, Jimmy."

It was the first time the marshal had used Jimmy's nickname. "There might not be one offered yet," Jimmy replied.

"There will be," the marshal said. "The Union Pacific doesn't waste time. The Omaha bank is also offering a reward."

"There's something else here," Jimmy said. He was looking at a small pile of watches, rings, and gold pieces. He reached in and pulled out Mary Ann's pendant. "I'm sure this belongs to your daughter."

The marshal nodded. "It was my mother's."

They unsaddled their horses and made sure the animals had food and water. Then they walked back to the station. Mary Ann had helped Barbara bandage her neck, and now Barbara was fussing over Mary Ann, while Henry cleaned up the mess that had been made during the incident.

"I guess we're going to need three rooms, Henry," the marshal said.

"Well, I have the rooms, but I don't have any bedding," Henry stated.

Barbara interrupted. "We have enough bedding for this young lady." She smiled at Mary Ann.

Chapter Thirty-six

Marshal Bringham, Jimmy, and Mary Ann spent the night at Fort Morgan, sleeping almost around the clock. After a sumptuous breakfast prepared by Barbara, they set out on the road to Latham and Greeley. The next day they caught the Denver Pacific to Cheyenne, a short train ride.

The marshal notified the railroad that the thieves had been found, two killed and one captured by James Whipwell, and the money recovered. The railroad gave Jimmy a nice reward. He wanted to share it with the marshal, but Brink refused, saying truthfully that Jimmy had done most of the work and taken all of the risk. The marshal also hired Jimmy as a second deputy, and Jimmy followed the marshal everywhere when Brink was on duty, even on his own days off. Bringham was a good tutor for Jimmy, teaching him the same kind of maturity

Jimmy would have learned from his own father, had it not been for the friction between them. Jimmy didn't know how his life could get any better. It did, though.

Mary Ann decided that Jimmy was going to be the man in her life and made herself available to him whenever he called. Jimmy let things progress slowly, however. He didn't want Mary Ann to slip through his fingers, but he had much work to do. When there was nothing for him to do as a deputy, he was taking care of his horses and looking for a small piece of ground to start a ranch where he could begin breeding them. Mary Ann, having spent her early childhood on the prairie, took to Jimmy's horses easily, and the two of them often worked together.

After several weeks in Cheyenne, Jimmy sat down and wrote a long letter to his father. He told him of the train trip, knowing that his father had seldom left the farm. He described the countryside he had passed through: Chicago, the Mississippi River, the Missouri River and the ferry, Council Bluffs, and Omaha. Then he told him of the train robbery and his role in the pursuit and killing of the two outlaws. He told him of meeting Marshal Bringham and how much he had come to respect the man. He told him of being awarded a deputy's badge in Cheyenne and what the town was like. Finally he told him about Mary Ann.

Father,

I have met a wonderful woman. She reminds me so much of my dear mother, and yet there are differences.

She grew up on the prairie but was educated in New York. She reads and writes poetry, paints pictures so beautifully that they cause longing in all who gaze upon them, and thinks as highly of me as I do of her, if that is possible. She is brave and resourceful, as I found out during my pursuit of the outlaws, but is tender and kind to every living creature. I have asked her to be my wife, and she has agreed. We plan to be married next year in May. Although I know how busy the farm is at that time of year, I would be so happy if you and my brothers would come. I received a small reward from the Union Pacific, and I can pay for your railroad tickets and arrange your lodging. Please consider this request.

Your son,

James Whipwell

Jimmy also received a letter. It was addressed to *James with the horses, Cheyenne, Wyoming.* The return address was, *Penny Bradford, Omaha, Nebraska.*

The postmaster found Jimmy in the marshal's office and showed him the letter.

"Is that you, Jimmy?" he asked. "I couldn't think of anyone else it might be."

So much had happened since Jimmy had helped Penny on the train that he almost didn't remember her. "Oh! Yes, I think it is," he said. He opened the letter while the postmaster observed.

Dear James,

Please forgive me for taking so long to rite to you. When I left Ogallala I rode all night on your good horse, and the next day I found my husbind Abe lying on the side of the railroad trak. He was bad hurt but alive. The man Ed Hollister had pushed him off the platform. We flaged down the eestboun train and rode back to Omaha ware he spent a week in bed under a doctor's care. He is getting stronger each day and gets around a little now. I hav my old job back, and that helps.

I hav too apolegies to make. I promised to return your horse and hav not been able to do so because of paing the doctor and the pharmacyst. I am taking good care of him, and I hope soon to be able to give him bak.

Also I apolegize for lying to you. Abe Jackson is not my husbind. I hope this does not disgust you, but we hav lived together as man and wife for sevral yeres. Becaus of all the recent evints we hav decided to get married and liv a mor normal life.
Yurs trule,
Penny Bradford

Dear Miss Bradford,

I am glad to hear that Abe is going to be all right. He and I had several delightful conversations on the train, and I thought of him as a friend, in spite of our short acquaintance. Please offer him my best wishes for his speedy recovery.

I am very happy to hear of your coming marriage. I, too, am getting married. I found and rescued the girl I met on the train, and we plan to be married next spring.

The horse you rode away on is named Golden. I would be very honored if you and Abe would keep him as a wedding present.

You owe me no apology for your relationship with Abe. It's better to be married, of course, for a number of reasons, but true love is the only thing that really matters, as I have found out.

Sincerely yours,

James Whipwell, Deputy Marshal

Cheyenne, Wyoming Territory